Emeline

A Journey

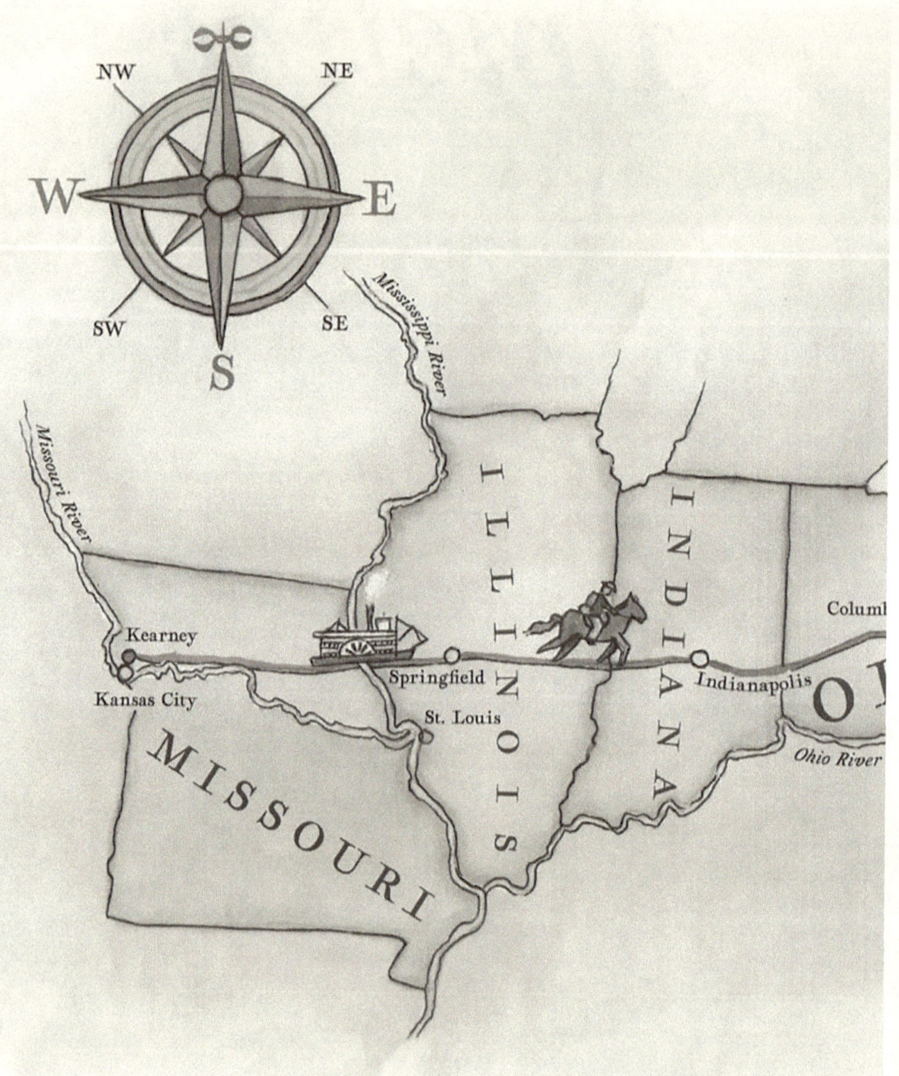

NW
NE
W
E
SW
SE
S
Mississippi River
Missouri River
ILLINOIS
INDIANA
Columb
Kearney
Springfield
Indianapolis
Kansas City
St. Louis
O
MISSOURI
Ohio River

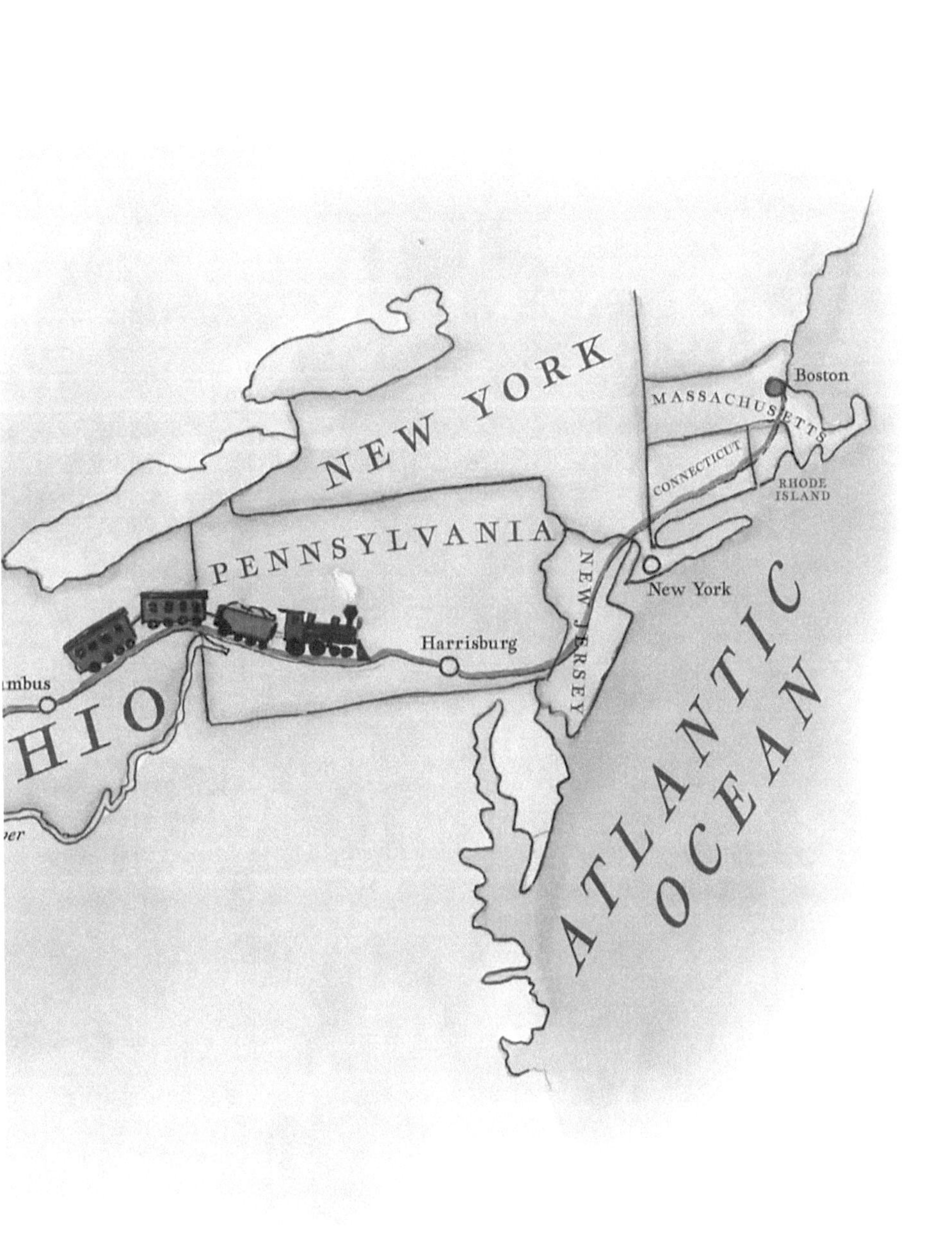

NEW YORK
MASSACHUSETTS
Boston
CONNECTICUT
RHODE
ISLAND
PENNSYLVANIA
NEW JERSEY
New York
Harrisburg
OHIO
mbus
ATLANTIC
OCEAN

Emeline

A Journey

KATHY J PERRY

Dedicated to my daughters:
Cassidy Anne and Emily Danielle

May you be confident, courageous,
resourceful, self-reliant and never forget
that the Lord is with you always.

Acknowledgements

This book would not have been possible without the wonderful instruction from Dan Schwabauer and his OYAN (One Year Adventure Novel) curriculum, which helped me with plot, characterization, and structure. Thank you, Dan.

Jeff Gerke's books *The Irresistible Novel* and *Plot vs. Character* were immensely valuable also. Thanks for the encouragement to "not be boring".

The KCWCW (Kansas City West Christian Writers) group members gave encouragement and support all along the way. Even when I thought the rough draft was finished, Cora Allen's critique gave me insight and suggestions, which changed the book dramatically.

Thanks to my editor, Beth Bruno who, with love and long hours, gave constructive criticism and corrections, giving the book a professionally polished appeal.

I feel fortunate to have found such an artist as Claudia Gadotti who took the story and some visual cues from me and created the most beautiful artwork I could have imagined. The first edition did not include these lovely illustrations, but I still used them on bookmarks and promotional materials. Some thought illustrations would not appeal to young adult readers. I disagree now.

Rebecca and Andrew Brown of Design for Writers creatively designed a new cover and interior for the second edition of A Journey. It has the same look as designed by the original designer, Rachel Lawston of Lawston Design. This edition features all of Claudia's illustrations, although printing costs force them to be in black and white. They're still amazing! Thank you.

Thanks to Abigail VanTerry, the narrator for A Journey's audiobook experience. She embraces the tough challenge of both Boston and Irish accents, as well and mid-western speech dialects. Her voice talents bring the story to life. An outstanding treat for the ears!

Thanks to my family, who puts up with me and my seemingly unending work on the computer and provide support through encouragement, patience, and love.

And, finally, thanks to my Lord and Savior for giving me the vision for this story, and the next, along with abilities. It is my sincere hope this work pleases You and that many enjoy it.

Contents

Loss

The year was 1890. I was thirteen, soon to be fourteen, and in my last year in our one-room schoolhouse. Handwriting was next: I carefully wrote the assigned verse: Matthew 5:3.

Blessed are the poor in spirit: for theirs is the kingdom of heaven.

I blotted tears with my sleeve so I could see to write.

Miss Ambrose stuffed the wood stove with several short pieces of split oak. The remaining embers caught the new wood on fire. Warmth seeped throughout the one-room schoolhouse and nipped the early spring chill. She sashayed past me, her two petticoats rustling beneath her white cotton dress; the heels of her leather boots clicked the wooden floor rhythmically.

She reminded me of Ma. She even smelled like Ma - all clean and soapy. Also like Ma, her hair was partly braided and swept up into a large bun at the back of her head. I set my piece of white chalk into the groove on the desk and whisked away more tears as memories of her flooded my mind.

Miss Ambrose placed her hand gently on my shoulder. "Would you like to visit later?"

"Yes, ma'am, for a little while," I answered as my hazel eyes met her blue ones. Since Ma passed away in childbirth, Miss Ambrose has been like a second mother to me.

"Class, it's time for lunch," she announced. "Henry, please fetch some water for us. John, will you bring in more firewood please? Thank you."

Row by row, we lined up like ducklings to retrieve our lunch pails and cups from the shelf over our coat hooks. We dipped our cups into the bucket of fresh water Henry brought in and returned to our seats. "Yum." Fresh bread, sliced cheese, and an apple lay wrapped inside a cloth napkin.

Then we could talk! "How are you, Emeline?" asked Harriet. My friend and neighbor spooned some ham and bean soup into her mouth. "Mmm. I'm so hungry."

"I'm well, thank you. I'm excited to farm with Pa this summer. The past few summers I've shuttled the looms at the wool mill, but this year their business is slow. How 'bout you?"

"I'm not sure yet. We might be moving to Westport."

"No!" I exclaimed.

"I don't want to, but Dad applied for a construction job there. He's always liked building things with brick and wood. He says if he gets the job he'll sell the farm and earn more money, though the work is hard and the days long." She stirred her soup.

"Change is hard, isn't it?" Not wanting to dwell on the possibility of my best friend moving away, I switched subjects. "After lunch, let's ask Sarah and Charlotte to play double Dutch with us. Want to?"

"Sure, I love double Dutch," she said. "We're not certain yet that he'll get the job anyway; so no sense tormenting myself about it now, I guess."

We polished off our lunches, rinsed our pails outside in the cold water spilling from the pump, and set them back on the shelf along with our cups. Outside, the sun radiated warmth overhead, announcing the promise of spring, even though the air chilled my fingers and toes.

School continued as usual the rest of the day and, after the other students had left, Miss Ambrose seated herself across from me. "Okay, Miss Emeline, what's on your mind?" She smiled and folded her hands in her lap, attentive.

"Thank you for spending time with me, Miss Ambrose. I understand you still have work to do." Her eyes were expressively kind and welcoming.

"I miss Ma so much. I think about her all the time."

"I guessed that might be what was weighing you down. Why don't you recount your favorite memories of her?"

Stuffing my hands deep in my pockets, I let my mind recall two years ago. "It's so hard!" Tears welled up in my eyes. I soaked them up with my sleeve and pulled at the loose, wavy tendrils of my dark brown hair.

"Think about how dear she was, and why. It's important and healthy to talk about her, you know. As long as you can recollect her, she's never completely gone," Miss Ambrose said softly, offering to hold my hand. I held it tightly. "What did you admire most about her, Emeline?"

"Her kindness. And patience. She taught me so many things: how to put up green beans and other fruits and vegetables in jars, how to make apple butter, and how to sew. I stitched up the dress I'm wearing now." I paused, smoothing the gathers in my skirt with pride. "Sometimes she got angry, but never for long. Both Ma and Pa taught me to love God; we took turns reading chapters from the Bible in the mornings. I can keep a house neat and clean. Oh, and she shared stories about her life as a young girl. Those are some of my best-loved times with Ma."

"Those are valuable memories, Emeline. You should write them out in a journal. Describe all the memories you can. By doing this, she'll always be a part of you. You'll be stronger that way because her strength will join yours. Try it and see."

I sighed and smiled, "Thank you for listening. I will try that."

"You're welcome, Emeline. Visit with me anytime after school." We rose from our seats. She escorted me to the door and watched me cut across the schoolyard to the road leading home. She waved and called out, "See you tomorrow!"

I waved back. Tomorrows. Not many more of those until school will end for me. It's a good thing I have Pa as my rock. How would I manage without him?

4

Tavis O'Connor wiped the sweat from his brow, even though the air felt cool. The big, hundred-year-old oak fought him for its life. Its large roots, like knobby fingers, spread from its base, gripping the earth. The massive tree grew taller than any other on the farm; one man couldn't reach all the way around its girth.

"Come on down, Mr. Oak," he said. "We need your wood and you're in the way in this field." Tavis drew up his axe again with his rough, burly hands to chip out a "V" on the trunk of the tree; the chiseled angle became deeper and wider with each stroke.

Soon he heard a pop. "Yaw! Give it up. It won't be long now, Dakota." The Morgan horse nickered and nodded his head while he pawed the ground. He pushed against the tree after a few more strokes with the axe.

At last the tree gave way. Creaking and groaning, it fell flat into the field. "Whoop! There she is." Tavis celebrated with a long drink of water from the barrel strapped to his wooden cart. "Ach." He gripped his left arm; a dull pain had stopped him short. "What's this?"

He sat down in the soft soil of the field. "I wish Dad could see me in this farm life," he said. He pulled the gun his dad had given him from its holster and stared at the engraved initials on both sides of the handle: TO on one side and SO on the other. "He understood why I didn't want to stay in the city and work for his lithography company. Too stifling."

He remembered his wife, Kate, whom he missed terribly, and how they had agreed to stake a claim here through the Homestead Act of 1862. "We had so much fun building up this farm together." He wiped his eyes with his sleeve.

"I'm worn out. I'm gonna need neighbor Bob's help and Emeline's to saw this mammoth into pieces." Once the mysterious pain subsided, he climbed up to the bench at the front of the cart, held the reins, and clicked at Dakota to move out.

Back at the modest, whitewashed farmhouse, Tavis unhitched Dakota and removed his harness. He walked to the tack room of the barn with him, hung up the harness, and picked up a currycomb to clean the dirt and sweat from the horse's back. He then tucked him into his stall for a feeding of hay and oats, along with some fresh water from the well. Milking the bellowing Nellie, their beloved Jersey cow, was next.

At last he entered the house and collapsed on his bed to sleep. The aching pain had subsided. "All I need is sleep." And so, he rested until Emeline came home from school.

I walked lightly on the dirt road toward home and thought about what Miss Ambrose had said. 'Write down all you can remember about your ma; her strength will run through you.' My steps quickened. Ma had given me a journal that I hadn't written much into yet.

A fat red-breasted robin hopped along in the grass beside the road and paused every few steps to feel the movement of worms beneath his feet. "Spring is surely near if you're here, Mr. Robin," I said to him. A fluffy-tailed gray squirrel chattered by his nest high in the treetop.

Hiking up and down rolling hills, my body warmed even as the sun sank lower in the sky — a golden disc slipping out of sight. Watercolor pink and orange splashed color throughout the clouds stretched across the evening sky as I arrived home.

"Pa, where are you?" I found him sleeping on his bed. "Good. I'll fix supper while you rest."

Embers from earlier in the day still glowed in the wood stove. Tying my apron on, I added more chunks of dried split oak from the pile near the front door. Out front, I pumped water into a bucket and returned to pour it into a medium-sized, black, cast iron pot on the stove. Shortly, the fire burned hot and was ready for cooking; the water in the pot boiled. From the food safe, I selected a choice bit of beef, sniffing it for any foul odor. None found, I smiled and sliced it into bite-sized chunks and put them in the pot.

The root cellar, an underground room near the house, held our fresh vegetables. In the blue light of dusk, I lit a lantern and took it with me, along with a basket over my arm, and opened the cellar door. The air smelled musty yet good at the same time. I collected some potatoes and carrots in the basket. Back in the kitchen, I cut the vegetables into pieces and added them to the stew, along with some onion cut off from the braid next to the stove. Sprinkling in some salt, I said, "There."

Next, I mixed up the ingredients to make biscuits: milk, a bit of butter, cream of tartar, a pinch of salt, and enough flour to make a stiff dough. I kneaded the dough well. I pushed and pulled the ball of dough, turning it at quarter-turns just like Ma taught me. "Look for the slight tears in the dough," she had said. "Then it's ready to roll out." I rolled it out flat, cut the biscuits out with a glass, placed the circles of dough on a flat metal baking sheet, and slid it into the hot oven. "These will be ready shortly."

Once done, I pulled them out, and covered them with a towel to keep them warm on the stovetop. Supper filled the little house with a sumptuous aroma.

My stomach growled as I smoothed my apron and checked on Pa. "Pa?"

He rolled over and opened his eyes. "Oh, hello, Emeline. Good day at school?" He sniffed the air. "You've made supper?" He stretched. "How long have I been asleep?"

"You must've been exhausted, Pa. I visited with Miss Ambrose after school for a little while. Did you fell that big oak today?"

"Yaw. It took most of the day, but, yaw, it's down. I'll need Bob's help to saw it into pieces, and your help to split it. We'll burn lots of it, but some pieces I'd like to mill into boards. Miss Ambrose is kind, isn't she?"

"She is most kind. She understands my sadness about losing Ma." Our eyes met.

"I know. I often think about your ma. Kate and I had fine times even through the trials during the move from Boston and settling this land. She is with the Lord now and watches over us. You remind me of her so much. I'm glad you're here, Em."

"Yes, we still have each other." I paused, thankful to be compared to Ma. "Well, supper's ready. Let's move to the table and eat. You must be hungry!" I served up the stew and biscuits and put some salt and butter on the table too as I waited for him to come into the main room. He didn't seem quite himself tonight.

He swung himself up and planted his feet on the wooden floor. Standing, dizziness overcame him and he fell back to sit on the bed. "Whoa, that was too quick." Slowly this time, he got up and walked gingerly to the table. "The stew looks and smells delicious! Biscuits too? And, butter! Thank you."

"You're welcome," I said. We both ate, but I ate more than Pa.

"I'm not sure why, but I'm not feeling well, Em."

"You overdid it today," I said. "Chopping down the oak tree was probably too much work for one person. I'll save the leftovers for you in the food safe once cooled. Why don't you go on back to bed? I'll come in and read to you shortly."

"Sounds good," he said.

I followed him as he pressed himself up from the table and shuffled toward the bed, crawled under the coverlet, and pulled it up to his chin. "I am grateful for Kate's handiwork," he said. He ran his fingers over the intricate stitches in various colors. It gave beauty, warmth, and good memories. The down pillow comforted his head too.

With Pa safely snuggled in, I cleaned up the dishes and put up the leftover food. From the bookcase, I picked one of his favorite books, *The Adventures of Huckleberry Finn.*

Lantern in hand, I pulled a rocking chair close to his bed and opened the book to the first chapter. Pa looked at me.

"I love you, Em," he said.

"I love you too, Pa." As I read, I noticed his chest rising and falling with each slow and deliberate breath; his blue eyes almost closed. I remember Ma used to read or tell stories to me until I slept. I began:

> *"YOU don't know about me without you have read a book by the name of* The Adventures of Tom Sawyer; *but that ain't no matter. That book was made by Mr. Mark Twain, and he told the truth, mainly."*

At the end of the first chapter, I gazed at Pa's handsome, though weather-worn face. He slept with a slight snore. "You pull too much weight, Pa." I kissed his forehead and placed the book in my apron pocket to read another chapter later. "Love you."

I'll have to launder Monday, I thought, as I changed into my nightgown and tossed my dirty clothes in the pile of others needing washing. I read chapter two from The Adventures of Huckleberry Finn by the lantern until my eyelids grew heavy. I snuffed out the light with a yawn and fell asleep.

Our rooster crowed at dawn Saturday morning, waking me from a long, adventurous dream. Rubbing my eyes I said, "Morning already?" Reality dictated I get up and prepare for the day. "Ooh, this floor is cold," I said as my bare feet hit the floor.

I threw on my robe and wanted to stoke the fire in the wood stove to warm the house. But first, I checked on Pa. "Pa?" No answer. "Pa?" He couldn't still be asleep, could he? Drawing closer, I understood from his wincing face that he was in pain; it was hard for him to even breathe.

"Oh no, Pa!" I sat on his bed and held his hand. "What's wrong? Can I get a doctor for you? Don't leave me, Pa!"

"Em. No time. It's my heart." Tavis grimaced as he spoke with labored breaths. "Please. Take my Bible. Stay with my dad in Boston. Your grandfather. Silas O'Connor. Lithographer. Remember?"

My body shook uncontrollably, but I held in tears as I listened. "Yes, Pa. Anything else?"

"Promise me. Let him get to know you – love you as I do. Family is important." He stopped to gather what little strength remained. "Take the gun he gave to me. Initials on the handle – his and mine. Proof of who you are. Tell him I love him." His last words were, "Have courage. Don't forget, God will be with you. Love you, Em." His breathing stopped.

So did mine, for a moment. The life in Pa, once so strong, was gone. He would join Ma with Jesus in heaven now. I had never felt so alone.

Friends

With my arms wrapped around Pa's arm, I sobbed. I knew he would want me to pray. "Dear Jesus, I know my parents are both with you now. I want them to be proud of me. Please show me the way. I need You. Amen." I stood up, wiped my face with my robe, and gathered my strength.

I built up the fire in the wood stove again and waited for the rooms to warm. "What will I do without you, Pa?" I thought of my friends, neighbors, and my schoolmarm. Miss Ambrose. *She will help me.*

I filled the washbasin with fresh water and splashed it over my face. The cool water felt refreshing on my hot, red, and swollen eyes. After cleansing the rest of myself, I dried off and got ready for the trip.

Clad in my last clean dress and pantelettes, a pretty ivory outfit with small rosebuds all over and a sage green sash Ma made with me, I laced up my leather boots and pulled my wavy hair back and tied it off with a matching sage scarf. I gathered my coat and gloves and tied on my hat. "I'll be glad not to have to wear a coat in a few weeks."

Thoughts whirled through my mind as I approached the barn. Nellie bellowed for me. "Oh, Nellie! I almost forgot about you. Milking must go on." After this chore and throwing some feed at the chickens, I put up the milk, washed my hands again, and then readied Dakota for the trip.

"Hello, Dakota, my friend. It's only you, Nellie, the chickens, and me now."

The horse whinnied and pushed his face into mine as I slipped on his bridle and bit, his cobalt blue-striped woolen saddle blanket, and his leather saddle. I waited for him to release his held breath so I could cinch it tightly.

Dakota was a Morgan horse, shorter than other breeds, so I could easily reach the stirrup with my boot. We started at a walk, then increased our speed until we were at a full gallop. Pa had taught me to ride. "Pa…" I let the tears come and they vanished in the breeze.

I stopped by Harriet's house first, but their buggy was gone. "Where are you?"

A few minutes later, Dakota and I arrived at the little white house next to the school. I dismounted in an instant, tied him to the white picket fence post, and shouted, "Miss Ambrose! Miss Ambrose!"

The front door swung open, and Miss Ambrose pushed open the squeaky screen door. "Yes? Oh, hello, Emeline. Is something wrong? Please, come in." With a wave of her hand, she invited me into her parlor.

"Oh, yes, ever-so-much. Pa passed away this morning." My swollen eyes still stung as they searched her face for comfort.

"Oh, no, Emeline! What happened?"

"Um," I cleared my throat. "He said it was his heart. I was with him at the end. He worked especially hard yesterday, and with his last words he gave me instructions and I made promises to him. I don't know what to do first, Miss Ambrose. Can we talk?"

"Of course." She sat in her rocker. "First, let's pray." I fell to my knees on the floor next to her feet and we held hands as she said, "Dear heavenly Father, thank you for all you do for us each day, and for giving us days to help each other and, thereby, honor you. Today, we mourn the passing of Tavis O'Connor, who is with you now. Give us direction, strength, and the comfort only You can give. Hear our cries, O Lord, and give us peace and direction. Amen."

We rose. Miss Ambrose said, "I'll put on some water to boil for tea and cook raisin-oatmeal for our breakfast. You haven't eaten, have you?"

"No, ma'am."

"Will you pull the oats, salt, sugar, cinnamon, and raisins from the pantry, please? The tea things are on the table already."

I gathered the ingredients and brought them to the kitchen while Miss Ambrose placed two cups, bowls, and spoons on the Battenburg lace placemats on the oak kitchen table. Soon, the smells of breakfast filled the air.

"How hungry I am! Thank you, this is delicious." The warm oatmeal with raisins tasted sweet and filled my empty stomach.

She poured hot water into my teacup, and I placed the tea ball with black leaves into it, letting it steep. After a minute, I removed it and set the ball onto the saucer.

"I have to tell you about the last moments with Pa," I said. I informed her about promising Pa I would travel to Boston to get to know Grandfather Silas.

"That's a very ambitious idea, Emeline. I know you're intelligent enough and can do most anything you set your mind to. But what will you do with the farm?"

"I don't know. Maybe sell it? I'll ask Mr. Pickwick at the mercantile if he knows anyone looking for one.

"Hmm," she said. "How about your immediate plans for the funeral?"

"After I see Mr. Pickwick, I'll drop by the funeral director's parlor and make the arrangements." I paused, and thought how different things had been yesterday. *'Have courage' Pa had said. I don't want to disappoint him.*

"I'm so sorry, Emeline." Miss Ambrose reached across the table and covered my hand with hers. "How can I help?"

"Since it's Saturday, if you're not too busy, I would enjoy your company on the trip to town."

"I can manage that. Let's clean up and we'll get started. We can take my horse and buggy."

"Thank you. It will be nice to spend time with you."

Soon, we were nestled together on the small seat of her buggy. Light and easy to pull, the buggy had a bit of spring to it that helped smooth the ride over the ruts in the dirt road. Her gentle horse, Winnie, was a beautiful dapple gray mare with a black mane and tail.

"But, first, let's pray"

On the way we talked about my favorite times with Pa, like I had done only the day before about Ma. "Pa always acted like such a strong, tough leader, yet he had a tenderness of heart for Ma and me, and almost any animal. He told me he and Ma had come all the way from Boston to put down roots and develop the land they acquired through the Homestead Act of 1862. City life didn't agree with Pa. Why, when they first arrived, there wasn't anything on the land at all! They basically camped on it, while working the land until it produced crops that would both feed them and give them money to build. It took several years to complete the house. Then I was born." It felt good to remember, but it was bittersweet. "Pa taught me how to hunt with a gun, how to fish with a pole, and how to use lots of tools. I'm a pretty quick log splitter. My journal will be well-used in the coming months."

"I'm glad." Miss Ambrose looked at me and smiled.

The sun warmed up the day; a slight southwest breeze encouraged the birds to come out to visit one another. Twittering and chittering filled the trees and announced the approach of spring. Miss Ambrose smelled fragrant. She wore a soft, musky scent along with a pink calico dress and straw hat. She had wrapped a dark pink ribbon around her hat and tied it into a bow in the back that hung over the brim.

The door squeaked for oil as we opened it into the mercantile. Busy with people buying food, fabric, and sundries, a tall, stout man of about 40 years stood behind the counter.

"Hello, Mr. Pickwick," I said with my head held high. "I've come to see if you know someone who might be looking to buy a farm."

"Emeline, why would you ask me such a question?" he asked.

Confidence lost, I looked at the floor sadly and said, "You see, Pa died this morning. His heart gave out." I looked up at him.

Miss Ambrose put her arm around my shoulders.

"No! Tavis O'Connor?" the storeowner asked.

I nodded.

"We traded for supplies only a couple of days ago. He looked healthy as you please." With true sorrow reflected in his brown eyes, he said, "I'm so, so sorry, Emeline. He turned toward a young woman behind the counter. "Deborah, will you take over for me, please? I need to speak with these folks." He gestured to a little table in the back corner of the store with four wooden stools. "Come, let's sit at this table."

I looked around the shop at all the customers. Most were shopping. One man waited near the doorway, watching for someone, I presumed. My eyes shifted back to Mr. Pickwick. We gathered our dresses and sat upon the stools.

"Mr. Pickwick, we," I stammered, "I mean, *I* have a nice farmhouse with a barn full of hay and corn and one hundred sixty acres of fertile farmland that's mostly ready for planting. The house has a pump and well outside and a nice wood stove inside. We also have a Jersey milk cow, Nellie, and several chickens. Plus, there's a cart and numerous tools and things. I'm keeping the horse, Dakota. I can't stay here. Even if I could, I couldn't run the farm myself, so I need to see if I can sell it. I'm traveling east to meet my grandfather and will need some money. I promised Pa I would go."

"Do you know anyone looking for property?" asked Miss Ambrose.

"Let me think." Twisting the ends of his mustache, Mr. Pickwick said thoughtfully, "Well, I heard some men talking the other day about land," he said, looking around as if one of them might be standing nearby. But, he continued, "There's a new man in town named Ben Turner who's in the market for a place. Then there's Rod Simpson; he's *always* looking for a good deal. And, I believe the pastor knows of someone too. Why don't I talk to each of them for you and arrange for a showing, to be held after the funeral. Then you can ask for bids and take whichever one you please."

"What do you think, Emeline?" Miss Ambrose asked. Her eyes connected with mine.

"Thank you." I held my breath and summoned my courage again. "That sounds like a plan. Shall we say in a week's time, I can show the property?"

"Splendid. I'll meet you at your place with interested parties next Saturday – say ten o'clock in the morning," said Mr. Pickwick. "And, again, Emeline, I'm sorry for your loss. I will miss Tavis, too. He was a good friend and a great man."

Down the street was the funeral director's parlor. My eyes took a moment to adjust to the dimness inside. An ornate fireplace with a table in front of it stood in the center of one wall. Fancy chairs were placed around the room for guests. Victorian style, flocked wallpaper adorned the walls, while heavy, dark red velvet curtains gilded with gold edging hung dramatically from two closed windows. A small piano occupied one side of the fireplace and a stand, from which I suppose someone would speak, stood on the other. In a musty corner behind this, a candleholder in the shape of a cross promised hope. Dark and claustrophobic, the elegance of the room with its dank, stale air, held no interest for me – at all. Quiet, I stood with my hands stuffed in my pockets.

"Welcome," said the director. "My name is John Pendergast. How may I serve you?"

Miss Ambrose started the conversation, sensing my discomfort. "Thank you, Mr. Pendergast. Emeline has lost her father as recently as this morning and she needs help with the burial services, please."

Tears welled up, but I refused to allow them to fall. *Courage. Pa said I must have courage.* Drawing myself up straight, I said, "I'd like Pa buried next to Ma please."

"I'm very sorry to hear your sad news," he said politely. "Yes, we can take care of the burial for you. Would you like to have the service and visitation at your home and then have a burial at the cemetery?"

"Yes, please. A simple service will be fine," I said, taking a step back.

"Alright. We'll be over this afternoon to make the necessary preparations. The service will be performed after the customary two days: Monday at two o'clock in the afternoon. Please invite all those you wish to attend. And, don't worry about the expenses. We can handle those after your affairs are settled. We'll keep it as low as possible."

"That's fine." Miss Ambrose handed Mr. Pendergast a slip of paper she had written on. "Here's the address."

Why didn't I think to do that? "Thank you, sir," I added, and turned toward the door. Now, it was official. Pa's body would be buried next to Ma's.

"What an emotional day." With a heavy sigh, I breathed in fresh air and stepped up to the buggy seat. I glanced at the bustle of people doing their business up and down the street as Miss Ambrose climbed on board.

"You're welcome to join me for supper, Emeline, and you can spend the nights until after the service if you like. I've got some ham and beans we can warm up, and we can bake some fresh cornbread tonight."

"Sounds delicious, and thank you for the invitation. I accept. But I'll need to milk Nellie first," I said. "And, Dakota, Nellie, and the chickens will need to be fed. May I also bring my laundry to do before the funeral?"

"Yes, you may. I'll get supper ready while you ride home and take care of the animals. Dakota can stable with Winnie for a few nights." She guided her horse out into the road and we drove back to the house, weary and peacefully quiet. Leaning next to her, my eyes closed for a much-needed rest.

After we arrived at her house, I rode Dakota home to feed the animals, then stopped back by Harriet's. They were home this time. I knocked on the door and she answered. Just looking at my face made her come outside. "What's wrong?"

"Oh, Harriet!" I cried. "Pa's gone. He passed away this morning from a heart attack."

"No! Oh, Emeline." We hugged each other tightly as I cried into her shoulder; which was exactly what I needed.

The Big Day

After the funeral, I prepared the house for inspection and gathered the needed supplies for the trip. Soon the men would be coming over.

"Oh, Dakota, you're such a good boy. I'm glad we'll be making this trip together." I stroked his neck as I led him to the fenced pasture. One of his ears twitched and turned to listen. He nickered softly. "You'll need a new set of shoes before we leave." Then, I heard the approach of several men on horseback.

"Hello, Miss Emeline," Mr. Pickwick said, dismounting and taking off his hat and pointing to each man in turn. "These gentlemen are Mr. Ben Turner, Mr. Rod Simpson, and Mr. Logan Cooper. They are all considering purchasing your farm."

"Good morning and thank you for coming. After you tie up your horses on the hitching posts, I'll show you around."

As I gave the tour around the farmyard and inside the house, I noticed each man's manner and attitude. Not that it really mattered all that much, but I didn't wish to sell the farm to someone I disliked.

Mr. Turner asked many questions about things, like, "Can I take a sample of your well water and have it analyzed?" *Water is water, isn't it?* I thought. Was he trying to find fault so he could offer less? His suit was impeccable and looked very expensive. *Was he even a farmer? I wondered.*

"Fine by me," I said. "What do you expect to find? It's good well water - fed by a spring, Mr. Turner."

"One time I bought some land that had water that was full of arsenic. That's a poisonous metal, if you don't know." He pumped some water into a little jar and screwed a lid on it. "You have a pretty little place here."

"I like it." Secretly, I hoped he didn't.

Mr. Simpson didn't say much, but he touched everything, checking for sturdiness, I guess. He had a long face that looked pinched, like someone had taken both sides between their hands and pushed them together. But he was polite and even smiled now and then.

"Do you have any questions, Mr. Simpson?" I asked.

"No, not yet." He banged on the pipe from the stove to the ceiling to see if it was secure, I suppose.

What if it wasn't? What if it fell over and he got a face full of soot? I chuckled at the thought but said nothing.

"Everything is safe, Mr. Simpson. You'll find my Pa took good care of everything mechanical and structural."

"Hmph."

Mr. Cooper wore overalls and, of the three, looked most like a farmer. He asked good questions too, like "How many acres are there?" "How many gallons of milk does your Jersey give?" and "How many eggs do you collect each morning from your chickens?" He looked to be in his thirties and healthy.

After I answered his questions, I asked, "Why do you want this farm, sir?"

"My wife and I just moved here from Wisconsin, and we're looking for a place to grow a few crops and raise some dairy cows. Maybe someday we'll have a family too," he said, thumbs under his overall straps, as he looked out over the pasture at Dakota. "How about the Morgan? Does he come with the farm?"

"He's the only thing I'm taking with me, Mr. Cooper. He's a good workhorse, but I have need of him. The farrier in Kearney probably knows of other horses for sale though." I liked him.

After all three men looked over the farmhouse, barn, and furnishings, they climbed back on their horses to ride around the property with Mr. Pickwick, who knew the borders. Then they came back to the house. I wondered if they'd have more questions.

"Thank you, Miss," said Mr. Cooper. "I will talk it over with my wife and make the best offer we can."

I smiled. "You're welcome, sir."

Mr. Simpson lifted his hat toward me, and rode away. I didn't expect more from him.

"I'll test this water sample and make you a fair offer. Thank you for your hospitality." With that, Mr. Turner rode off as well.

"Each man will meet with me on separate appointments at the mercantile this afternoon. I'll bring you their offers later, Emeline – about four o'clock" said Mr. Pickwick, as he shook my hand.

In a few hours, I would have offers on the farm! *I hope
Mr. Cooper has the best offer,* I thought. In the meantime, I took
inventory of the supplies I needed to pack:

In my pockets:

- Pa's compass, Pa's pocket watch, a few coins for food or supplies

Around my waist:

- Pa's knife in its sheath, Pa's gun and gun belt, money belt
  (under my clothes)

Hanging from the saddle:

- Two water canteens

In my rucksack:

- Pa's Bible, mess kit, matches and fire starter, my journal,
  pencil, and money clip
- Bag of food (lots of jerky, nuts, raisins, apples, carrots,
  cheese, bread)
- Toiletries (hairbrush, hair ties, toothbrush, toothpaste, bar of
  soap, washcloth, and two small towels)

In my pack behind the saddle:

- Small tent
- Short shovel
- Axe

- Two blankets
- Clothes (1 dress, 1 extra riding outfit, boots, socks, hat, gloves, coat)
- Currycomb for Dakota

Pa's watch ticked softly in my pocket. *Tick, tick, tick.* I gazed over the horse pasture while a soft breeze caressed my face; four o-clock seemed like forever. "Hey, Dakota. Let's go see if Harriet's home."

Dakota whinnied and ran up to the gate.

I led him to the tack room and got him ready, careful to curry him before I put on his blanket and saddle. "I hope she's home this time."

We traveled down the road for about two miles. When we arrived, Harriet was outside painting the fence around the front of their house.

"That looks nice," I said, riding up and flinging myself off Dakota.

"Oh, it's you - my best friend," she said glumly. She put her brush full of white paint across the top of the paint can.

"What's wrong?"

"Nothing. I'm sorry, Em. I should be kinder to you since you've just lost your pa. But, I can't help feeling sad about losing you. Do you *really* have to go to Boston?"

"I understand. Well, I will miss you too, Harriet, but I have to try, don't I? I promised," I said. "Tell you what. I'll send you letters as I'm traveling. And when I get someplace that I'm going to stay for awhile, I'll send you my address so you can write me back. How does *that* sound?"

"Better than nothing, I guess. Are you ever coming back though?"

"Can't say yet. Just getting there is a lot to think about. Maybe. Pa said family is important and I have to keep my word."

"What if you didn't? He wouldn't know. You could stay here in Kearney. There are lots of people who could help you run the farm. Please think about it. If you leave, I'll worry about you the whole time."

"Number one: Pa will know about it. He is watching me, even now. Number two: I'm too young to run a farm – even with help. I'd have to sell it or something and move in with you. That part would be fantastic though."

"Yes! You could live here with us. Oh, please say you will!"

I hugged my friend and smiled at her. "Tempting as that is, I still can't forget my promise to Pa. And, I actually want to see where Pa and Ma came from. Even if I fail miserably, I have to try, no matter what the cost."

Harriet sighed. "I don't want you to fail, but I do want you to come home someday. I'll pray for your safety all the time you're gone." She turned back to the paint can and grabbed her brush. "Want to help me finish painting? I have an extra brush."

"Sure, I'd love to help," I said. We chatted and laughed, and remembered old times like when she and I dressed up in costumes and put on a play for our parents.

Time flew by and then I remembered. I checked Pa's watch: 3:30 p.m. "Oh, I need to get home. Mr. Pickwick is bringing the bids on the farm soon."

"Alright. Thanks for the help. Come tell me what happens. And, don't leave without saying goodbye!"

I mounted Dakota and headed home. "Bye! See you later," I said.

"Bye!" Harriet waved.

"I have some interesting news for you, Emeline. All three men want the property, but one didn't bid," Mr. Pickwick said.

"Which one?"

"Mr. Cooper."

"Aww, fiddlesticks. He's the one I hoped would buy it. He reminded me of Pa," I said.

"Well, I have bids from Mr. Turner and Mr. Simpson both. Mr. Turner's bid is higher, but still low for your farm, in my experienced opinion."

I gave my two cents worth. "Mr. Turner doesn't seem like a farmer at all. Not by the way he acted and dressed, anyway. What would a man like him do with the farm?"

"To hear him tell it, he wouldn't farm it at all: not the way you would expect. Your estimation of him is accurate. His interest is in the development of the land into a neighborhood of homes that he would rent out or sell to people for a profit. A farmer of people, you might say. A city fella."

"Pa wouldn't approve of that! He and Ma labored and invested their life savings to build up this property as a *farm*."

Mr. Pickwick continued. "Then there's Mr. Simpson. He's not a farmer either, as he's too old. He wants to buy it for his son and daughter-in-law's family."

"Do you know anything about them?"

"Not much. However, I have seen where they live and how they take care of that house. I can't recommend them. No."

"Oh dear. I can't travel without money. What should I do?" I spoke more to myself than to Mr. Pickwick. Then an idea came to me. "I wonder if the Coopers could stay on as caretakers with you as manager. Would you manage the property for me, Mr. Pickwick?"

He rubbed his chin and twirled the ends of his mustache as he usually did when he was thinking. "That's a definite possibility. Good idea, Emeline! They can live there, care for the animals, and any new animals they bring on, as well as plant and harvest the crops. They could stay for free and collect the majority of the earnings, giving you twenty percent and me five percent at the end of every year. That might be an agreeable compromise."

"Yes!"

"I'll draw up a contract and we'll propose it to the Coopers. If they agree to the terms, we'll then open a new bank account in the name of 'The O'Connor Estate' for you. Speaking of the bank, you should check with them. I'm sure your pa deposited money there."

"I had forgotten that!"

The next morning, I rode into town to check with the bank, and, sure enough, Pa had saved a good deal of money in his account. The banker heard Pa had passed – as did everyone in town. Pa was a popular man. So, he allowed me to withdraw some funds for my journey. I took enough in case I needed to take a train or for some unfortunate event: fifty dollars. "I'll make a money belt for this, but now I'll just put twenty-five dollars in each of my boots," I said.

No one else was in the bank, but the banker said, looking around, "Never show anyone how much money you carry. Come into my office and divide it there. And I'll make five dollars of it in quarters, dimes, nickels, and pennies for you."

"Thank you, sir." After securing the paper money and coins in various places in my clothing, I walked over to Mr. Pickwick's office next door. "Good morning!" I smiled.

"Good morning, Miss. Are you ready to suggest your solution to the Coopers?"

"Yes."

"Since they're new to town, they're rooming at the inn temporarily. They'll sure be surprised to see us!" Mr. Pickwick laughed.

After greeting us at the door, Mr. Cooper let us in and we explained the offer. "Really?" Mr. Cooper said. "That's too good to be true! What do you think, Sarah?" he asked, looking like a kid at Christmas.

"We can't pass this chance up, Logan," his wife said as she looked around their small, but tidy, room. "Oh, I'm so excited to move in!" She jumped up and clapped her hands around mine. "Thank you, Miss Emeline."

"God bless you," I said. "This is so important to me. I'm confident you'll take good care of it. And, I'll write to you and give you my address when I arrive in Boston."

"Sounds like we have an agreement," said Mr. Pickwick. "I've drawn up this contract. Please review it and if you have any questions, just ask me. If it's satisfactory, then both of you can sign and date it at the bottom and we're done."

After the farm deal, I asked Mr. Pickwick if he knew where Ole Mr. Thompson lived.

"I surely do," he said. "Follow the main road north for about two miles, then head right for another three. Are you familiar with the Henderson place? The big yellow house?"

I nodded.

"That's where you turn. You can't miss it. Look for lots of wood stacked around and pups running around loose," he said. "Tell him I said howdy."

"Okay. Thank you!" I turned to leave.

Ole Mr. Thompson is an old, old man who has lived in Kearney for nearly 30 years – even when it was called Centerville! I wouldn't be surprised if he might have had some Indian friends.

His house didn't surprise me: a small dwelling with puppies playing in the yard, just as described. The mother dog was sleeping on the porch floor next to a rocking chair occupied by the old man with his head hung over – apparently napping the warm spring morning away.

Not to disturb him, I played with the puppies for awhile; the feisty little pups yapped and rolled playfully. Soon, he awoke.

"Hello, Mr. Thompson," I said.

"Good morning. Do I know you?"

"You knew my Pa, Tavis O'Connor. You helped him on his homestead many years ago when he and ma, Kate O'Connor, first came to Kearney. Remember?"

"Oh, sure, sure, yes. I do recall. How are good ole Tavis and Kate?"

"Pa's in heaven with Ma, Mr. Thompson. We just buried him yesterday and Ma died two years ago. I'm their daughter, Emeline. Pa told me many stories about you and how you helped them get started." I shared the promise and planned trip with Mr. Thompson. "I'm hoping you will teach me survival skills I might need on the road, please?"

"Alright, missy."

"Emeline."

"Miss Emeline. Be right back." He rose from the chair, shuffled into the house, and returned with two tall glasses, which he filled to the brim with cold water from his pump in the front yard. "Here you go." He handed me a glass and returned to his rocker as I sat on the steps. Holding up his glass he said, "This is the most important thing you need. It's number one. Water."

"I'm listening."

"You've got to drink some water at least every three or four hours while you're awake. You can take some with you, but if you run out, what will you do then? Hmm?"

"Get some from a lake or a creek somewhere." I said.

"That's one way. If you do that, you've *got* to boil it to kill all the bacteria and germs. Otherwise, you might get sick. And how will you boil the water?" he asked.

"I guess I'd have to stop and build a fire," I said.

"Yep. That's right. Do you know how to build one? A good, hot one? One you can set a pot on? One that's not obvious from the road? You don't want to be robbed or killed, do you?"

"No!"

"Didn't think so." He took a long stick and played with it in front of the pups as they tried to get it. "Besides water from a creek or such, where else can you get water?"

"I don't know. I'm probably not likely to run into a well, am I?"

"No," he laughed. "Not likely. Well, there's rain. You're bound to have wet weather somewhere along this trip. It's a long, long way to Boston, young'n. When it does happen, stop and seek shelter under a tree. Stretch a piece of slicker cloth across some low branches, or if you have a small tent, that'll work. Use your mess kit pan to catch rain water that will drip down into it and then pour that water into your canteens. And, you've got to have more than one of those, you know. Rainwater is perfectly safe to drink. Ain't no need to boil it."

"Oh! That's good. Especially since it would be hard to build a fire in the rain."

"Even if it doesn't rain, do the same thing at night. When you camp down, the overnight dew will drip down into your pan. It ain't much, but it's something. Now. Grab that shovel over there and come to the back of the house." Mr. Thompson ambled to the back, grabbing his fire starter from the porch railing.

"Thank you, Mr. Thompson," I said, following with the shovel.

"I'm going to show you how to build a fire in a hole," said Mr. Thompson. "Find yourself a spot off the road, down near a big tree with smaller trees growing underneath – or some bushes. Clear the leaves and twigs from the ground there and start digging." He cleared a place and pointed.

I started digging. "How wide and how deep?" I asked.

"About a foot across and about a foot deep," he said.

After that was finished, I said, "Now what?"

"Now you need to dig another hole," he said.

"What?"

"Yep, you need air coming in through the bottom, so you dig a smaller hole next to it – just as deep. Then use a knife, or spoon, or even a sharp rock to dig out the dirt between the two holes at the bottom – like a tunnel."

After this was done, he continued.

"You'll need three types of kindling. Number one: cottony stuff, real light, you know, like milkweed. No milkweed in spring though. You could even use a scrap of cloth. Number two: dried grasses. Number three: dried needles or sticks. Then, you make a bird's nest.

"A what?"

"A bird's nest, like this, see…" He laid needles down first, then topped them with grasses. Finally, in the center, he put a cottony material. Then he picked it up and bent it into sort of a circle and placed it in the bottom of the hole. "There. Now you use your matches or fire starter to light the cottony stuff."

Flames ignited everything in order. "While this is burning, find yourself some small sticks and lay them on top, then bigger sticks. Then broken branches. Finally, if you want to cook on it, go to a small tree and cut off some skinny branches with your knife and peel the bark off of them. The green wood won't be quick to burn. Lay several across the fire, criss-crossed, like a grid and put your pot of water or your pan of fish, or whatever on it. If we were by some small trees right now, you would notice that the smoke would filter through the leaves and branches and not go up like this column here does. Your fire won't likely be seen because of smoke."

"Go on!"

"Now, when you're done with the fire in the morning, just use your shovel to push the dirt back into the holes and spread the leaves around. It'll look like you were never there."

"Thank you, Mr. Thompson. I will definitely use this skill on my trip. Is there anything I can do for you?"

"Stay safe, young'n. If you will, just send me a card when you get to where you're going. That'll be thanks enough. Wish I could ride along with you, but I'm too old and tired."

"That's alright. You take care of yourself. Thanks again!" I unhitched Dakota and rode home to prepare for tomorrow's departure.

Departure

Packing took nearly a whole day. But, now I was ready. My oiled canvas pup tent served well to wrap most everything dry and together. My oil cloth rucksack held smaller items, including food, my canteens filled with water, Pa's Bible, compass, and watch. Its straps went over my shoulders and around my waist to balance the weight. Under my clothes, I wore a money belt with twenty-five dollars, but I also put twenty dollars in the rucksack, and five dollars in change in my rucksack's outside flapped pocket. My riding skirt had a belt with Pa's knife sheathed and clipped to it, along with Pa's shortened gun belt and gun lower on my hips.

I looked around the house one last time, for it would never be the same again. "Mrs. Cooper will enjoy Ma's Singer treadle sewing machine," I said to the empty room. All the patterns, notions, machine oil, and the like peeked out of a box next to it. Smoothing my hand over the oak table, I looked at the stove; many a good meal would be served here again.

Before I became too melancholy, I went out to feed the chickens and Nellie one last time. I patted the Jersey's neck and looked at her big brown eyes. "Such long eyelashes. You'll like the Coopers, Nellie. They'll take great care of you and even give you some companions soon."

Dakota surprised me with a velvety soft muzzle nuzzle; he nudged me as if to say, "Let's go."

"All right, let's get you some new shoes." Stepping in the stirrup, I swung myself up, sat comfortably in the saddle, and gathered the reins in both hands. "Okay, giddy'up!"

"I'm really doing this!" I said. On our way to Kearney, we stopped by Harriet's, Miss Ambrose's, and even Ole Mr. Thompson's places to say goodbye.

The farrier was not far from the mercantile. "I'd like a whole new set of shoes for Dakota, please."

"You're the boss," said the farrier. "That'll be $4.00 and about an hour's time."

"Thank you," I said. I took off my rucksack and gave him the money. "I'll just be in the mercantile saying goodbye to Mr. Pickwick."

"Fine. Be ready soon."

In the mercantile I said, "Hello, Mr. Pickwick. I'm just stopping by to say goodbye."

"Good morning, Emeline."

"Mind if I have a little breakfast here and pass the time while I'm waiting on the farrier?"

"No, please do. What can I get you? Some hot tea and pastries, or maybe you'd rather have some bacon and eggs?"

"Bacon and eggs, please, and some tea would be lovely."

"Coming right up."

It was early, so not many shoppers were in the store yet.

"This is delicious! What a send-off. Thank you."

"Good-bye, Miss Emeline. Godspeed. Do send a letter or card from time to time so's we'll know you're all right. We'll worry about you something fierce."

All loose ends tied up, it was now time. Because I knew Pa and Miss Ambrose would want me to, I prayed. "Dear Jesus, please be with us on this journey and keep Dakota and me safe. Thank you. Amen."

Once out of town we headed north toward the next town of Cameron at an easy stride. The dirt road was clear and mostly straight with a few trees on either side. We rode over hills and down through valleys. The blue sky had the prettiest wispy white clouds high above us. Breathing deeply, the fresh air felt amazing. I'd never felt so free; like I had the whole world in front of me where anything was possible. "Dakota, would you like to hear a song?"

His ears twitched and turned back toward me.

"Alright. Ma used to sing this to me; it's one of my favorites."

Lavender's blue, dilly, dilly,
Lavender's green
When I am king, dilly dilly,
You shall be queen.

Who told you so, dilly, dilly,
Who told you so?
'Twas my own heart, dilly, dilly,
That told me so.

Call up your men, dilly, dilly
Set them to work
Some to the plough, dilly, dilly,
Some to the fork.

Some to make hay, dilly, dilly,
Some to cut corn
Whilst you and I, dilly, dilly,
Keep ourselves warm.

Lavender's green, dilly, dilly,
Lavender's blue
If you love me, dilly, dilly,
I will love you.

Let the birds sing, dilly, dilly,
And the lambs play
We shall be safe, dilly, dilly,
Out of harm's way.

I love to dance, dilly, dilly,

I had the whole world in front of me
where anything was possible

I love to sing

When I am queen, dilly, dilly,

You'll be my king.

Who told me so, dilly, dilly,

Who told me so?

I told myself, dilly, dilly,

I told me so.

I took in a deep breath and exhaled. The fresh air cleansed my lungs and filled me with hope. Dakota cantered along, content with the weight he carried and the long dirt road that cushioned the impact of his hooves. We were making good time and nearing our first stop already: Cameron, Missouri.

I pulled Dakota over to the grass and dismounted. We'd traveled for about two hours and deserved a rest. I heard a trickle of water in the distance. "Let's go get you a drink. Good boy, Dakota."

Holding his reins, I led him through the open field to a creek gurgling with water from the spring rains. It felt good to stretch my legs and do some bending side to side. Dakota lowered his head and drank deeply. Afterward, he pulled up and munched on tender grasses with a nicker as if to say, "Thanks".

From my rucksack I took out my first canteen, guzzled about half its water, and snacked on a stick of deer jerky Pa had made. The spices he used made the meat tasty, but it was tough and took

45

awhile to chew. I didn't fill my canteen with water from the creek, as I knew we would be in Cameron soon and I could do so there from a pump. Later, there would be time to build a fire and boil water, if need be.

"That's enough. Let's get moving, Dakota," I said, remounting. "We'll stop for a few minutes when we get to Cameron."

Thankful for the pristine weather, I took notice of all the little signs of spring on the way: small buds on the trees, tiny green shoots of grass along the road, the first leaves of tulips, and even purple crocus blooms. I hadn't seen anyone on this road since I left Kearney so far. I whistled a little tune for Dakota. His ears pricked and turned to listen.

Then, around a bend, I saw farmland, houses, cattle, and horses. Some farmers were working in their fields. Closer still, I saw the town buildings and we slowed down to a walk. "Hello," I said to a stranger on a horse going the opposite direction.

"Howdy!"

He took another look at me after he passed, I noticed. *Maybe he wonders why a strange young girl is out riding by herself.*

We walked through the main street of town toward the mercantile. I dismounted and tied Dakota to the rail next to a horse trough in case he wanted more to drink. A pump outside the mercantile filled up my canteen again. I thought I'd just wander inside for a look around. Pa had come here before, but I never had.

It wasn't much different. Same kind of folks shopping and talking together; close neighbors. One tall man in a white hat with his back toward me peered over his shoulder to look at me several times. Feeling uneasy, I bought a little bit of hard candy to suck on, put it in my rucksack for the trip, and left the store.

We walked the rest of the way through town and turned eastward toward Chillicothe – and eventually, Boston. Running once more, we didn't get too far before I heard the rhythmic sound of hooves behind me. Was this someone in a hurry to get somewhere? My imagination took a trip around the possibilities. "Heyaa!" I dug my boot heels into Dakota's ribs. Now he was galloping as fast as the wind.

But the other rider was still behind me, and the distance narrowed between us. A short way up the road, I saw another road that led to a farmhouse. "Ho," I told Dakota. He slowed to a trot; his breath deep and quick. I pulled off the road and waited for the other rider to pass me.

But he didn't! "Hey, little girl, what are you doing out here all by yourself?"

It was that man with the white hat from the mercantile! "On my way home," I said, pulling Dakota away from his horse and walking him toward the farmhouse.

"I've never seen you before. You got any money on you?" He leaned over and snagged Dakota's halter with one hand to stop him. He grabbed my leg with his other hand and tried to pull me off.

"NO!" I screamed and kicked him as hard as I could. "Let go of my horse!"

He grinned, dismounted, and tried to pull me off again. "I bet you've got money in there. Let's take a look."

I kicked his face as hard as I could with my left leg, pulled out Pa's knife, and cut the hand that was holding Dakota.

"OW! Why you little…" His brow furrowed, his lips curled, and his eyes glared at me. Blood ran down his hand and onto the dirt. "Come here!"

"Get away!" I screamed again. "Hayaa!" I said to Dakota, who broke loose and galloped up to the farmhouse.

Hearing the ruckus, a man ran out who had been working in the barn next to his house. Using his red kerchief, he wiped his brow and said, "What goes on?"

"Sorry, mister, but I had to pretend this was my house. That man was trying to rob me, and maybe more." I looked back at the road. The man in the white hat was headed back to Cameron, his hand wrapped in a bandana.

"That man?" the farmer asked.

"Yes, sir."

"I know that man. That's Jeb, and he's a bad egg. He's been in jail lots of times. You were lucky to get away. You must have grit."

"Grit or not, I need to get back on the road. I thank you for your help."

"Sure you don't want to come in for a bit?"

"No, thank you. I'm fine now." I caught my breath. "Got many more miles to travel today."

"Alright. You be careful." He waved goodbye.

Once we were miles away, we relaxed once again. I patted Dakota. "Good boy. We're safe now." He snorted.

Sometimes, we would see a rider or farmer working, but nothing out of the ordinary. I'd offer a friendly wave as we passed. We needed to get through the next large town of Chillicothe before we could rest at our first night's stop in Marceline, Missouri. Miss Ambrose wrote to a friend who lived there, telling her that I would be stopping by sometime. This was the only stop where I would have such a luxury.

Every couple of hours, I would get off, stretch my limbs and walk Dakota for a mile or so, making sure he had opportunities to drink, graze, and rest for awhile too. But most of the time we traveled, we alternated between a comfortable walk and a canter gait. We didn't stop at Chillicothe at all. Today's destination was so close.

It was evening when we reached Marceline. A full eleven hours of travel in one day. Both Dakota and I were ready to take a long break. Miss Ambrose told me exactly where her friend, Miss Douglas, lived. She was just west of town, by the school, in a little white house next to it. Finding the school was easy; it was right off the main road.

We made our way up to her house, I dismounted, tied up Dakota, and stretched again. I walked up the path to the bright yellow front door and knocked.

Miss Douglas opened the heavy door and then the squeaky screen door. "You must be Emeline. Miss Ambrose told me you would be coming this way. Please, come in."

"May I take care of my horse first?"

"Yes, by all means." She pointed. "There's the stable over there with my horse in it. There's plenty of hay, feed, and water for him."

"Thank you." Dakota groaned as I took the bundle off his back full of my supplies, followed by his saddle and blanket. From the pack, I pulled out his currycomb and brushed the sweat and dirt from his back. "You have been such a wonderful traveling companion. Get a good night's rest. Tomorrow's another long day for us. Good night, Dakota."

I looked at the warmth coming from the house. The yellow door was open with just the screen door shut. I could see inside the main room to a rocking chair where the teacher was busy knitting. "Hello, Miss Douglas," I said as I entered the room. "Thank you for letting me stay here tonight."

"Hello, Emeline. You're welcome. How was your trip today?" She put down her knitting and motioned for me to join her at the kitchen table. "Before you answer, have you had anything to eat?"

"Just some deer jerky Pa made, an apple, a piece of cheese, and water," I said as I sat on an oak chair at the table.

"Well, I have some leftover vegetable beef soup and some biscuits. How does that sound?"

"Heavenly, just heavenly. I appreciate your feeding me and allowing me to spend the night."

She put some of the soup into a small pot to heat up on the stove. A plate with two biscuits, a knife, and a pat of butter were placed in front of me. A small pot of honey with a drizzling stick caught my eye on the table. "I haven't had honey in a long time." My mouth watered in anticipation.

"Be my guest, Emeline. We have lots of apiaries here. Honey is an inexpensive commodity. If you like, you can take a jar with you."

"Oh, I dare not. I already have quite a load for Dakota to carry."

She brought over the bowl of soup and took a seat across from me. "Now, tell me of your trip so far."

"Mmm. This soup is delicious." As I ate, I shared the events of the day.

"Oh, dear, Emeline. You could have been killed by that man!"

"I was very glad that the farmhouse was so near. In the heat of that moment, I just wanted to survive and get away. My fears dissolved into action."

"Well, even so, I know Miss Ambrose would advise you to have a companion for the next part of your journey. I have a good friend, Mr. Spencer Phillips, who travels to Hannibal on business frequently. In the morning, let's ask if he's available. You can trust him, and traveling together will keep you safe."

"That would be lovely, and I would enjoy his company too." Still hungry, I asked, "Would it be possible to have another bowl of soup, please?"

"Surely." Miss Douglas poured the rest of the soup into the empty bowl.

The steam rose to the delight of my nostrils. My belly now full, fatigue washed over me. My heavy eyelids blinked away the extra water from my eyes.

"You need sleep. I'll prepare a pallet for you on the floor." She stacked two heavy blankets on the floor plus a beautiful, hand-made quilt with fan shapes in various pastel calico fabrics, and finally, a feather pillow. "Before you bed down, let's pray."

"Yes, please."

"Why don't you start, Emeline."

I wasn't used to starting. "Dear Heavenly Father, I'd like to thank you for everything you've done for us, and everything you will do. Thank you for the deliverance from that man earlier today. Keep me safe on my journey to Boston. And, thank you for Miss Douglas, her hospitality, and her suggestion for travel with Mr. Spencer Phillips. Amen.

"Amen. Now, off to bed. We'll have a nice breakfast in the morning before you leave."

"Thank you for everything. Good night, Miss Douglas."

Crossing the Mississippi

At first light I pulled out my journal and pencil and wrote:

Thursday, March 20, 1890

Yesterday, Dakota and I traveled from Kearney to Marceline. I learned to be wary of strangers and discovered I could defend myself. I miss you, Pa and Ma, but I'm determined to continue until I meet Grandfather Silas.

After I washed and dressed, I read Matthew 5:4 for my devotional and prayer time. Quietly, I let the words speak to me, much like when Pa read them aloud.

"Blessed are they that mourn: for they shall be comforted."

Then I prayed: "Thank you for these words. I miss Pa so much, but I know he is with you in heaven with Ma. Keep me close to you, as I know Pa and Ma would have wanted. Amen."

"Good morning, Emeline," Miss Douglas said. "Help me with breakfast?"

"Yes, how can I help?"

"Collect the eggs from the henhouse, please. We'll have scrambled eggs, warm cinnamon-raisin bread, sausage links, and milk."

"Yum! I won't take long," I promised, grabbing a basket near the door.

Miss Douglas grinned as she cooked the sausage links and sliced the loaf of bread.

Still cool, the sun was bright and promising. "Good morning, Dakota!" I passed the barn to the henhouse and collected eight brown speckled eggs from the clucking hens. "It's alright, I'm just visiting," I said to the birds. "Thanks for the eggs."

I delivered the basket. "Anything else?"

"Yes, you can pour two glasses of milk. The food safe is right here." She pointed to a familiar box frame with galvanized screen mesh on the sides and door. Two shelves held perishable foods like milk, butter, cheese, and meat inside.

"We had a Jersey dairy cow back home. Her name is Nellie," I said, pouring milk from the glass bottle into two small glasses. "I hope she'll be alright with the Coopers."

"I'm sure she will be. Breakfast is ready. Come and eat."

I took my place at the table and Miss Douglas said grace. I filled my plate with the food she'd prepared. "I don't know if I've ever eaten better food. The raisins in this bread are so sweet." I ate greedily.

"It's funny how much better things taste after a hard day outside, isn't it? But I do like this bread, very much. My mother taught me how to make it."

"Miss Ambrose told me that if I remember Ma, she'll always be part of me. And, just like your mother, you are still making that same bread."

"Yes, that's right. How is Miss Ambrose?"

"She's fine. I'm glad she sent me to your house for the night."

"Me too, Emeline." After breakfast, she said, "Let's go see if Mr. Phillips can accompany you. He runs the mercantile in town. Every week he travels to Hannibal to pick up more goods and supplies." She drank her milk. "The Father of Rivers, the Mississippi, is a major trade route from the east, north, and south parts of the country, you know."

"Yes. We studied it in school. I'm excited to see it. Just think, I'll be crossing that big, old river soon!"

We cleaned up the dishes, got our horses ready, and rode to the mercantile in Marceline. The main street was as pretty as you please; rows of neat brick buildings lined the dirt road with large picture windows displaying their wares. Wood plank sidewalks held the many walking customers safely from the traffic of horses and carts of all descriptions. Presently, we met the proprietor, Mr. Phillips.

His hair was cut over his ears, naturally curly, and parted on one side. A young man, probably ten years younger than Pa, with a proper suit and tie, his manner and language showed he was well-educated. "Hello ladies, how can we help you today?" he asked.

"Hello, Mr. Phillips. May I introduce you to Miss Emeline O'Connor?"

I curtsied. He bowed.

"May we sit and visit?" Miss Douglas asked.

"Surely." He led them to a round table with three chairs at the front of the store.

Miss Douglas recounted my history to date and my purpose for traveling. "So, in the interest of her safe passage today, would you happen to be going into Hannibal? If so, could she accompany you?"

Leaning to one side, elbow on the table, and his head resting on his left hand, he replied, "I was going to go tomorrow, but I guess I could move my trip up by a day. If we're to do this, though, we must leave immediately. It's a very long trip by horse and wagon – two full days! If only the Santa Fe Railway went to Hannibal; but, alas, it goes north to Chicago."

"Are you sure it's no imposition?" I asked.

"No, no. It's fine. I'll just need to let the folks here know I'm leaving. We'll have plenty of time for visiting on the road. Give me an hour to pack and hitch up the team.

"Oh, thank you Mr. Phillips," both Miss Douglas and I said together. Miss Douglas' blue eyes twinkled as both our faces beamed with happiness.

"You're very kind," I said. "See you then."

The sun's promise held from this morning. It would be another wonderful day for weather. I had never traveled in a covered wagon before. Although this would delay my arrival by a day, I felt safe with Mr. Phillips, and also, it would be easier on Dakota.

"Get up, get up!" Mr. Phillips started the mules.

The mules, Abe and Clancy, were the color of nutmeg except for their flaxen manes and tails. Larger than Dakota and harnessed together, they pulled the prairie wagon easily while Dakota followed, tethered to the back of the wagon by a long rope.

Dakota's tack and my gear were stowed inside along with empty barrels and sacks from the mercantile. Other supplies for the trip included a cooking pot, a keg of water which hung on the outside, and some food. The wagon creaked and rattled over the road as it hit occasional rocks above the dirt's surface.

Mr. Phillips and I sat side by side on the front seat. "Riding in a wagon gives a body kind of a rest, doesn't it? Compared to riding horseback, I mean."

"Yes, it does."

"And with two people, one can go inside and sleep. If you like, I can teach you how to drive and I can rest for awhile; after I see if you can handle it, of course."

"Yes, please! I would love that."

"Watch those mules. See, when I pull the right rein, what happens?"

"They both go to the right."

"Now I'm pulling the left rein. What happens?"

"They both go to the left."

"Exactly. Easy as pie. There's a harness for the right hand horse and an exact opposite harness for the left hand horse. Then the right and left reins are fed through that little heart up there and switched between them; see it?"

"Oh, I see."

"There's a lot going on with a team harness; lots of straps and buckles and things you have to know when you're hitching them together. You have to be careful too, especially when you're hooking them up to the wagon. When the team is hooked up to the wagon - even just one of them - you have to be quick to get out of the way. If they move forward too much you could be run over by the wagon! Anyway, when the reins are switched like they are, then to go right, you just pull the right rein; and vice-versa.

"What do you say to make them stop?"

"I say, whoa or ho there."

"Alright. May I try?"

"Sure. It's a straight road to Hannibal."

I gathered the smooth, leather reins in my hands and tried leading them both left and right; just a little. "This is easy."

"They're good helpers, Abe and Clancy. I've had them a long time and they know this road as well as anyone. And, they're smart. A mule is different from a horse. I'm not taking anything away from horses, but if a mule is in trouble, he just stops until you come help him. If a horse is in trouble, he's bound to hurt himself trying to get out of it. Mules are sure-footed creatures and don't get frightened as much as horses, as a rule."

"They're magnificent."

"Mind if I play a little tune on my mouth harp?"

"No, please do."

Mr. Phillips pulled a silver harmonica from his pocket and began to play. Recognizing the tune as "Oh, Susannah", I sang along.

I come from Alabama

With my banjo on my knee,

I'm going to Louisiana

My true love for to see,

It rained all night the day I left,

The weather it was dry,

The sun so hot I froze to death;

Susanna, don't you cry.

Oh! Susanna, don't you cry for me,

I've come from Alabama with my banjo on my knee.

"I love music. It's especially nice out here in the wide open spaces; it comforts me."

"I'm glad. I like it too. I even brought my fiddle. When we camp tonight, I'll play it for us."

We drove on for miles, stopping every couple of hours where there was a nearby stream to water and feed the horse and mules. Unlike riding, we could drink from our canteens and snack while riding in the wagon, so we just stretched our limbs.

"Look behind us, Emeline."

A wall of clouds hung low and ominous in the distant west, though it was still sunny where we were. "Oh! Do you think that storm will catch up to us?"

"Depends on which way the wind's blowing." He licked his finger and held it up high. "Feels like it's coming straight east. Yep, it might catch us. We'll have to hunker down pretty soon, but we have a little more time."

"At least we have a covered wagon to protect us from the rain."

"That's true enough. I hope that's all it is. A covered wagon is no match for a tornado."

"Not a tornado!" I wondered where we would hide. And, what about the animals?

"Probably not. We'll have to wait and see, though."

"Get up Abe, Clancy, Heeya," he said, urging them to go a little faster now. Dakota brought up the rear.

About four o'clock, the wind took on a new personality. I pulled my coat from my bundle of gear, put it on, and cinched my hat up close.

"We'd better take cover." Mr. Phillips pulled the wagon off the road and headed toward a grouping of trees that signaled the existence of a small river or creek. Going over the prairie was a rougher ride than the road. We found shelter among the oak, maple, and pine trees. The wagon was situated so that the side was facing the oncoming storm, rather than the open front or back. He jumped down from the wagon and held his hand out to me. "Come on down. You'll need to water and tie up Dakota. I'll unhitch the team and take care of them. Then, we'll check all the wagon's cover ties and make sure they're tight."

"Alright." I jumped down and got to work. Lightning flashed inside the dense clouds, followed by loud claps of thunder and deep continuous rumbling as it rolled into the distance. I counted: "One Mississippi, two Mississippi" between the lightning bolts and thunder. "Two miles away," I said.

"Hurry!" Mr. Phillips said. "Get into the wagon now." We had tied all the animals up under the trees and all the ties were secure.

"I guess we won't be building a fire tonight."

"Ha! Right you are, but it's okay. I brought some smoked ham, cheese, and carrots. I even have some cake for dessert, and some herbal tea. If I fill our cups with water, the tea will make itself – even without being hot."

"Thank you, Mr. Phillips. I'm glad to have this wagon during the storm. I would have been standing next to Dakota otherwise. Do you think there might be a tornado?"

He smiled and looked at me with a sidelong glance as he arranged our supper on two plates. "No, not this time."

The rain came down in great drops and hit the sides and top of our canopy, but we stayed dry. "Poor Dakota, Abe, and Clancy." I took the plate offered me and began to eat.

"They'll be alright." He ate ravenously.

"What kind of cheese is this?" I nibbled it along with the slice of ham, savoring each bite.

"Mild cheddar. Do you like it? It's a best seller at the store."

"Yes, I do, thank you."

After supper, we enjoyed a piece of apple cake with cream cheese icing. Mr. Phillips had poured water and started the tea before, so it was ready to drink with the cake. "This is my wife's favorite recipe for cake."

"It's delicious." Chunks of apples moistened this sweet treat. "I love the cream cheese icing."

Though the storm raged outside, Mr. Phillips still pulled out his fiddle and began to play. Relaxing against my rucksack, I took off my hat, closed my eyes, and listened to the happy song of the fiddle with a backdrop of heavy rain. He played a rousing song to start: *Dance All Night with a Bottle in your Hand*. Then he played some slower songs, like "*Für Elise*" and "*Amazing Grace*." Between the rain and the music, I was soon asleep.

I dreamt about working on our farm, feeding the chickens, milking Nellie, and walking to school. Pa, Ma, and I sat around the table at supper while talking over the events of the day.

But something else was happening. Under my head, my rucksack moved and flaps were opened. Mr. Phillips knelt next to me with his hand inside the bag. "What are you *doing*?" Still sleepy, I sat up and looked at him. I saw him try to hide my money clip behind him.

"Nothing to worry about, just go back to sleep. I was just lying down for the night."

"No you weren't!" The haze of sleep was disappearing as adrenaline kicked in. "You stole my money!"

"Oh, this?" He pulled it out from behind him and held it out for me to see. "This is mine. You must be confused."

"I am *not*. I know my money clip when I see it." I grabbed for it, but he pulled it away quickly and shoved it in his pocket.

Looking for something, anything, I saw the cast iron frying pan near me. Fast as I could, I pounced on it, gripping its handle. My lips curled inside my mouth. With *all* my might I heaved that pan and hit Mr. Phillips over the head.

Dazed, he shook his head and looked at me. "What's the matter with you?" He tried to grab the pan from me, but before he could, I hit him again. He slumped over, unconscious.

"You're a thief!" I said, even though he couldn't hear my accusation. I rifled through his pockets and took my money back, put it in the rucksack, grabbed my hat, and threw all my belongings, including Dakota's tack, outside the wagon. I checked Mr. Phillips' breathing and heartbeat. He would be okay; he'd just have a bump on his head and a nasty headache.

I jumped out of the wagon and ran to the trees. "Dakota! We're leaving." I closed my coat tight, untied my horse, and brought him over to the wagon to saddle and pack him. The rain was steady, but the thunder and lightning had moved on. "I'm sorry I have to saddle your wet back, but at least the blanket is dry for the moment." I cinched his saddle, strapped on the pack with supplies, put on my rucksack, stepped into the stirrup, and we were off.

Because it was night, the road muddy, and still raining, I didn't want to ride Dakota too fast, so we used the extended walk gait. With lengthy steps, his back hoof tracks surpassed his front hoof tracks. "We should have a great lead from Mr. Phillips. He won't wake up for awhile, and when he does, if he decides to follow us, he'll have to harness and hitch up his team first. Even then, we can outrun them."

Dakota nickered and his ears turned back to listen to my voice. "Good boy, Dakota, good boy."

As usual, we stopped every couple of hours to rest for a few minutes. When we did, I opened my canteens to collect the rainwater in them as Ole Mr. Thompson had advised.

The rain slowed as morning approached. Tired and wet, I pulled my horse off the road toward a group of trees and a creek to rest. I needed sleep to keep going. I took off my rucksack and used it for a pillow on the grass.

After awhile, I woke up with Dakota's muzzle breathing in my face. It was still cloudy, but the rain had let up. Pushing his nose away, I said, "Alright, I'm awake. Let's go." Back in the saddle, we returned to the road and kept the same pace.

By noon, the sun and wind had dried the road enough that we could alternate between walking and cantering. I *must* reach Hannibal today, I thought, and get across the Mississippi before Mr. Phillips' arrival.

At last, I saw signs of Hannibal; houses and buildings appeared in the distance. When we arrived it was about four o'clock. We had traveled most of the night and all day, but we had finally made it.

We walked through the bustling town. We saw people visiting and helping each other load carts. Horses snorted and whinnied. Wagon wheels squeaked as they turned. There were bales of cotton and barrels of unknown contents. Some people looked at me and waved or said "Hey there." But I didn't stop. I continued east until I reached the Mississippi River. What a sight!

There on the wide river was a magnificent white and red steamboat. Never before had I seen such a boat! People carrying bags or boxes were walking across reinforced planks to board her; some walked their horses on board. Still others took their entire outfit, cart and all, on board. "Wow!"

Near the planks was a man dressed in slacks with a dress shirt and tie, and a fancy jacket with gold braided trim. He wore a special hat too. "He must be the captain, Dakota." We rode up to him and I dismounted.

"Hello, are you the captain of this vessel? And, are you going across the river?" I didn't want to go up or downstream by mistake.

"Yes, ma'am. I am. Looks like you got caught in the rain last night. Are you crossing?"

I must have looked a sight. "Yes, sir, I did get caught in the rain. And, yes, I'd like to cross, please. How much is the fare?"

"For a horse and rider it is $.50."

"Alright." I opened my rucksack and got the money from a little case of coin in the flapped side pocket. "Here you are."

"Very well. Go to the end of the boarding line over there."

"When will we leave?" I asked.

He looked at his pocket watch. "In about twenty minutes."

"How long does it take to cross?"

"Only about five minutes with this steamboat, Miss," he said with a smile.

"Only five minutes? That's amazing!" I smiled back.

"Here we go, Dakota!" We got in the line, which moved slowly onto the boat. The wooden boat had two tall stacks where the steam came out and was three levels high! I would stay on the bottom level as Dakota couldn't climb stairs. A huge wooden steering wheel peered over the top of the third level and would give the captain the best view. People lined the second level, while people and livestock occupied the lower one. Some looked over the side rails and watched the flow of the river.

I stroked Dakota's velvet nose and patted his neck. "We're safe from Mr. Phillips now. In just a few minutes, we'll be in a new state: Illinois!" I drew my map from my rucksack to refresh myself with my next day's route. "I hope tonight and tomorrow will be less troublesome. I can't wait to set up camp and get cleaned up."

I must have looked a sight. "Yes, sir, I did get caught in the rain."

Farms & Forests

When the captain came on board, the plank to the boat was unhooked and lowered to two small boats that took it to shore. Someone else on shore released the rope that was holding the rear of the ship steady. That rope was pulled in and coiled on the deck.

He climbed the stairs all the way to the top level to the ship's big steering wheel. Pulling a cord, the captain released steam through the two pipes whistles. Such a loud noise they made! The back of the boat had a big red paddlewheel that the steam engine turned to push us through the water.

First, we backed up, then, turning the ship's steering wheel, he signaled to switch the paddlewheel so we'd go forward. Crossing the Father of Rivers was easy as pie with this steamboat.

"Illinois, here we come," I said to Dakota. He whinnied and tottered to keep his balance as the boat moved through the strong current. The river was an odd color: muddy brown and olive green mixed. For miles up and down stream there were several steamboats navigating north or south. "It must take a lot of steam to go north against the current."

"It surely does, missy," a neighboring passenger said.

He had a horse and cart which carried barrels with lids filled with tools, boxes of nails, and boxes with bolts of colorful cloth. "Headed home?" I asked.

"Yep. Not too far."

"That's good." I smiled and looked at the coming shore. "Here we are, Dakota."

The steamboat pulled alongside the shore as two small skiffs brought over the plank and helped hook it to the deck. Then they maneuvered the other end to the shore and secured it. The long rope was thrown from the back of the ship to someone on shore who secured it to a post.

We disembarked, and I hopped back in the saddle. Pulling out Pa's compass, I held it until the needle lined up with the "N" for north. Then I looked for "E" for east. There were roads that led other directions, so I wanted to make sure I picked the right one. "Due east, that's what I want. The next town is Springfield, but we'll make camp before we make that journey, Dakota. Let's get to a good place for that." I clicked to my horse, then gave him the command for the extended walk pace. When clear of most people, we cantered for awhile.

Thankful for the progress – and the nice weather – we made our way deep into the countryside between towns. I looked for the clumping of trees and indications of water.

Straight ahead, over rolling hills, a row of trees grew thickly from north to south. The sun was setting soon. We needed to make camp. We rode until we reached the trees and left the road to find a solitary spot.

Dusk was upon us as the last amber rays of sun filtered through the woods and hazy evening air. I could hear wildlife: the last calls of songbirds, a slapping sound hitting water in the distance. What was that? Could it be a beaver?

"This spot looks good, Dakota. See, there are large trees with smaller tree growth under them, and no one in sight." I dismounted and gave my horse's neck a big hug. Then I pulled off the pack and canteens, removed his saddle, and hung his blanket up over a branch to dry. I pulled out the currycomb and brushed his back and haunches with it. He whinnied, stretched out his neck, and looked back at me with delight at this. He leaned into me as I brushed him, his eyes closing and his lips extended outward. "Feels good? I know, it's been a long, long time, hasn't it?"

Dakota still wore his bit and halter. I grabbed the bar of soap, toothbrush, toothpaste, and a towel from my rucksack and led him through the woods toward what I hoped would be water soon. Oh, how I wanted to wash up!

In just a few minutes, the trees opened up to sloping earth that met water – a lot of it! We had reached the Illinois River. Looking up and downstream, I couldn't see much, as the sun was disappearing and the shade of night was drawn down. But, I thought I might have seen a smaller ferry boat downstream. We would see in the morning.

For now, Dakota walked into the river, cooling his legs, and drinking great gulps of water. I took off my boots, gun belt, money belt, and knife and walked a few feet downstream from him. I stepped into the river. "Ooh! It's *cold*!" Not wanting to be shocked by the cold for long, I first brushed my teeth. Then I took the soap and plunged in, clothes and all. Scrubbing vigorously, I washed my body, hair, and clothes, all at once.

I jumped out of the water straight away and dried off as best as I could with my little towel, put my boots back on, and picked up the gun belt, money belt, and knife. Grabbing his reins, I said through chattering teeth, "Let's get back to camp, Dakota. After I change into dry clothes, we'll build a fire." Now full of water, he happily followed my lead. Back at camp, I used my rope to tether Dakota to a tree, allowing him enough rope to graze in a nearby clearing of grass.

I pulled out my spare riding outfit and laid it out as I disrobed. Shivering, I hung each article on a low branch to dry and put the dry clothes on; a pretty blue cotton blouse and khaki split skirt to wear over my money belt. Bending over, I brushed my hair from the back to the top of my head, and all around my head this way. I stood up and repeated the brushing. My hair felt clean and smooth and was drying in the night air. I was warming up.

"Time to build a fire." Sweeping away the twigs and leaves, I picked a spot under a small tree near a larger one and began digging my first hole: one foot wide, one foot deep. I piled the soft, rich soil close by. I dug the second hole about eight inches from the first:

half as wide, just as deep. Then I used my knife to hollow out a tunnel joining the two holes at the bottom.

"There! Now I just need my kindling." I collected some dry needles dropped by a pine tree, and small broken sticks, and a handful of dried grass. "All I need now is a bit of fluff." Certain there were no cattails or milkweed this time of year, I sacrificed my blouse by cutting off a bit of the bottom. "Now I can make my bird's nest." With care, I laid the sticks on the bottom, then stacked the needles, the grasses, and finally the bit of cloth. Bending and turning the components, the nest took its circular form and I placed it in the bottom of the larger hole.

From the pack, I took the firestarter and lit the cloth bit. Each part was engulfed in flame in turn. Immediately, I grabbed some sticks close by and stacked them on top, followed by bigger sticks, and then broken branches. "Ahh! That feels wonderful." I cut and stripped the bark off some green branches from the small tree and placed them criss-crossed over the fire.

Grabbing some food from my rucksack and my mess kit from the pack, I prepared my supper. I filled the small cup with water from my canteen and set it on the fire. I would have hot water to drink, which would warm me inside. Not having any fresh meat, I would have to be satisfied with deer jerky. A piece of bread, cheese, carrots, and an apple would round out the meal. "I'll have to get some more food in the next town."

My cup of water was steaming. With a towel wrapped around my hand, I took the cup off the fire, removed the grid of green sticks, and added small branch pieces. The fire was doing well. "I'm so glad

Ole Mr. Thompson taught me how to do this." I thought about him sitting in his rocking chair on his porch with pups playing in his front yard and smiled at the memory. I should write something.

By the firelight, I wrote in my journal:

Sunday, March 23, 1890
"Thank you, Jesus, for giving Ole Mr. Thompson this survival knowledge and leading me to him. And thank you for the crossing of the Mississippi and the safety of this night. Please be with us tomorrow as we continue our journey. Amen."

The night was clear and mild. I didn't think I really needed to put up the tent, so I just laid out the tent cloth on the ground, put a blanket on top of it, and followed with another blanket. My rucksack would be my pillow and I slipped between the blankets. Warm, clean, full, safe, and tuckered out, it didn't take long for me to drift off to sleep. The last thing I remember was Dakota's soft, happy nicker in the clearing.

A warm glow filtered through the trees and woke me up. I stood up, stretched, and yawned. "That seemed like no time at all. I slept so well." I pulled on my boots and picked up the shovel to fill in the fire holes with the pile of soil. Then I spread the leaves over the top. "Like I was never here." I folded and rolled the blankets up into the tent and stuffed it in the pack along with the mess kit and the shovel, and the clothes that had dried overnight. As I was packing my rucksack, I touched Pa's Bible. "Oh, I need to read today. I don't always understand what the words mean, but I know Pa would say understanding comes a little at a time. Keep reading, he would say." I read Matthew 5:5.

"Blessed are the meek: for they shall inherit the earth."

Afterward, I prayed again: "Thank you, Lord. Please be with me on this journey; keep me safe, and let Grandfather Silas be happy to see me. Amen."

Next, I pulled Dakota near the tack, lifted the wool saddle blanket from the branch, and centered it on his back. The saddle was next. Then I studied my map. Springfield was the next stop. "I can replenish my food and water there. I'd like to camp past Springfield tonight." I packed the map, put on my rucksack, and mounted Dakota. "Tch, tch, let's go."

We rode down to the shoreline again to let Dakota drink his fill. As he drank, I looked downstream and saw some kind of boat on the bank. There *was* a ferry! That was good news. I didn't know how deep this river might be or how strong the current might be either.

We walked the mile or so to the ferry. A man in overalls and a cap stood at the entrance in anticipation of his first customer of the day. "Hello!" I said.

"Hello!" he answered. "Need to cross?"

"Yes, please."

"That'll be one quarter for you and your horse."

"Fine." I dismounted and pulled the quarter from the side pocket of my rucksack and handed it to him.

"You go right ahead, Miss," he said, signaling me to board. "No need to wait. It may be awhile before the next folks come. Won't take long anyhow."

Dakota and I walked onto the deck of the little ferry.

"Stay in the center, now. To keep us balanced," he said. He put leather gloves on his hands. There was a heavy rope tied to the dock; the captain picked it up. It was strung across the whole river and tied up to a dock at the other side. There was a lot of slack in the rope so that it sank to the bottom of the river when it wasn't being used. He picked up the wet rope and pulled us across the river with his strong arms. Yes, it was slower than the steamboat, but still, a safe trip.

"Thank you, sir," I said as we arrived at the other dock.

"You're welcome, miss."

We walked onto the bank and he turned around to pull himself back again as no one was waiting to go west at the moment. "Safe journey," he said with a wave.

"Thank you." And, once again, we were headed east. As we walked along, I could see all kinds of wildlife: rabbits, squirrels, birds of all kinds, including a rafter of turkeys and one vulture. Springfield would provide me with food and water, but eventually, I would need to hunt or fish. When we cantered, I couldn't notice quite as much detail. The wind blew warm from the southwest; the sun rose high in a clear, blue sky. We rode downhill through valleys with fields of tall grasses, early spring flowers, and an occasional farmhouse with a barn and windmill, and we trotted through forests with oak, maple, and pine trees. We stopped frequently to rest, feed, and water Dakota.

By late afternoon, we arrived in Springfield. Much larger than anyplace we had been so far, most people were either home or headed that way. We walked through the main part of town in search of the general store, or mercantile. "There it is," I said to Dakota. On arrival, I dismounted and tied Dakota up to the hitching rail next to the horse trough of water. There was a loose bale of fresh hay on the ground under the trough. "Look, Dakota." He whinnied, immediately taking bites and munching contentedly.

I pushed the door open and entered. Because it was late in the day, few people were in the store. The proprietor asked, "Can I help you find something in particular?"

"I'm traveling. What do you have in the way of meat that can last on a journey?"

"Well, we have smoked turkey, smoked ham, and an assortment of jerkies over here."

"I'll take some smoked turkey and beef jerky, please."

"Sure," he said, preparing my bag. "We also have loaves of bread, cornbread muffins, apples, and carrots. Potatoes, too, if you want to cook them."

I smiled. "No potatoes this time, but I will take a loaf of the raisin bread, maybe six of the cornbread muffins, six apples, and two bunches of carrots. Is there a well with fresh water I can fill my canteens with?"

"Have a fresh water pump right here in the store, miss. Help yourself." He motioned to the front of the room.

"Thank you." While he finished my bundle, I looked around the store as I filled my canteens. Every wall had shelves with merchandise of some kind, like lanterns, bottles of oil, fire starters, and matches. Some shelves held bolts of women's calico and men's shirting and suiting material as well as an array of threads of various colors. Others held food staples like containers of lard, mason jars with preserved fruits and vegetables, and tins of preserved meats and fish like mackerel. Barrels held bulk food items like oatmeal, flour, sugar, and salt. On the counter was a large basket full of fresh eggs, and lidded jars with different kinds of sweets.

"Would you happen to have any eggs that are already hard-boiled?"

"Yes, miss, I do. How many shall I add?" He held his hand over another egg basket on the counter.

"Four, please."

"Alright. Will there be anything else?"

"Yes, I think I'd like a tin of mackerel, please. That will do. How much do I owe you?"

"That will be $1.40." He pulled the tin from the shelf and added it to the muslin bag.

I pulled the money from my rucksack pocket and handed it to him. "Thank you very much." I picked up the bag and returned to Dakota. I gave him one of the apples, which he crunched and slurped quickly.

Packing my rucksack with the new provisions, I checked my map for the next stop. "Camargo, Illinois. Right near the next state, Indiana."

Once again, we were on the road east. Outside of Springfield, there was a sign, much like a trailhead sign, pointing the way to different places. Finding Camargo's road, we headed east once again.

We stopped in just about an hour to make camp for the night. We picked a suitable location for Dakota's watering needs and protection from the road. I enjoyed a tasty supper, and the following morning had eggs for breakfast! The next morning I read Matthew 5:6.

"Blessed are they which do hunger and thirst after righteousness: for they shall be filled."

I prayed and wrote in my journal:

Monday, March 24, 1890
"Dear Heavenly Father, thank you for the safety of yesterday. I pray this day will be safe as well. I trust you, Father, for directing my paths and teaching me the right way to go. Amen."

Energized and excited for the day, I mounted Dakota and we continued for another eleven-hour day to Camargo, a smaller town. We camped again east of town. As my survival skills were becoming well-practiced, my confidence grew. In the morning, I read Matthew 5:7.

"Blessed are the merciful: for they shall obtain mercy."

I wrote my prayer in my journal.

Tuesday, March 25, 1890

"Dear Jesus, thank you for your Word. Help me remember to be kind and pray for those less fortunate or ill-tempered. Amen."

"Tonight we'll be in Indianapolis, Dakota! Another new state: Indiana." I patted his neck and gave him a carrot to munch. When he had chewed and swallowed it down, I mounted and we were off again. Could this be another good weather, safe travel day? I hoped so.

Like the last two days, the weather was pleasant, though windy. At least the wind was coming from behind us, which made our travels easier. My coat and hat kept me warm and protected as we traveled, alternating gaits and taking breaks as usual. The landscape hadn't changed much; we still came upon farms with fertile farmland for miles with intermittent forested areas. We walked through the small rivers and creeks easily. I had plenty of provisions, so I didn't stop to fish or hunt for more.

Occasionally, we would pass another rider or wagon on the road. I noticed the farther east we rode, the more people there were. Men tipped their hats and said, "Hello"; ladies nodded and smiled. I hesitantly returned their greetings with a smile. I didn't want to encourage any more familiarity at this time.

The morning and afternoon went on without incident, and I looked for a camping site for the night in the distance. "Dakota, that thick outcropping of trees at the bottom of the next valley looks promising." I knew I wanted to clean up and restock again in Indianapolis the next morning, so we would camp on the west side of it. "Maybe I'll even try to catch a fish tonight."

In the dusky part of the evening, I saw deer, two of which were fawns, feeding in the fields near the tree line. Canadian geese flew in a "V" northward bound in the now cloud-covered sky. "That's a good sign summer is on the way." I even saw a red fox for a fleeting moment as he dashed into the woods. The forest was becoming denser. The light underneath the hundred foot oak trees was dim as their thickness blotted out most of the sunlight. The canopy did not provide enough light for small trees to grow either.

I dismounted and led Dakota across a field and into the trees until we found the water at a good-sized creek. "This is perfect." The creek had a rocky bottom and a gradual incline to its bank. "You can drink your fill now, Dakota." I took the rope from the saddle and tied him to a nearby tree. The rope gave him plenty of opportunity to roam and forage for food. After I took off his saddle and blanket, I gave him a good brushing with his currycomb. He groaned with pleasure as he leaned into the brush.

This time, I did set up the tent. Because of the rocky ground, the tent poles were hard to set. I had to use my shovel to get a few of them in the ground. Then I dug my fire holes, collected tinder, and started my fire. I waited until I had sufficient wood on it for a nice-sized fire and laid my blankets inside the tent along with my rucksack. "There might be rain tonight."

From my pack, I pulled out the other split skirt and the red blouse; the same I had worn on the day of my departure. Though wrinkled, they were clean. I took off my boots and belts, grabbed the soap, sat down in the cool creek water, and washed myself all over - my body, my hair, and the clothes I was wearing. Teeth chattering, I then stripped off the wet garments and hung them to dry and hurried to dress again. I sat next to the now blazing fire and held my hands over it to warm myself. With my hairbrush, I stood, bent over, and brushed my hair thoroughly, upside down and then right side up, careful not to get too close to the flames. Satisfied with my progress for the day, I thought I might sing.

Just as I thought of a song, Dakota neighed and stomped the ground with his front hooves. "What is it, Dakota?" I thought maybe he was startled by an animal or something. I stood up, found Pa's gun, and ran to him.

Two men were standing by Dakota, smiling. "Hey there, little girl. Nice horse you have here," the taller one said.

Holding the gun out in front of me, I cocked it making an audible click. "Get away from my horse and leave us alone."

"Aww. Why so unfriendly? We don't mean no harm. We saw you come in here and just wanted to pay a friendly visit," the shorter one said.

"I don't believe you." I stood with my gun steady. "I don't want to hurt you, but I will if you don't leave." I noticed they both had guns too. I shot a warning shot at the feet of the shorter one and cocked the gun again. Startled, Dakota reared up and neighed.

The tall man used Dakota as a shield and walked toward me, while the other man hid behind a thick tree trunk.

"I'm warning you," I said.

But he cowered down behind Dakota. I had no clear shot.

He jumped from under Dakota's head and knocked the gun out of my hand. His big, rough hands circled around my neck, choking me. I couldn't breathe!

Health & Housekeeping

Nothing was familiar. What happened? I was in another place; not on earth. There was no pain. Everything was bright white and light. Beautiful music was everywhere. There was an indescribable and overwhelming feeling of love that enveloped my mind and heart. *"Am I dead? Is this Heaven? Oh, Jesus, if I'm dead, please take me."* I felt as if I were rising up, up, and up – almost flying. And I saw a hand and white-robed arm reaching down.

As suddenly as it had appeared, it was gone; melted away. I was jostling around in the back of a wagon. My belongings were there too. And Dakota was looking at me from behind the wagon. "What's happening?"

In the dark, a woman in a pretty, cotton calico dress sat next to me. "Shh. You'll be alright. You've been hurt." She adjusted a bandage on my forehead. "Samuel and I found you on our property. We're taking you to our house where we'll take good care of you."

Unable to control them, tears fell down my cheeks. I had lost that beautiful, miraculous moment and had returned to earth. The impact of such a moving experience is difficult to describe; almost unbelievable, yet it was *real*. Never before have I felt *anything* like that in my life.

"She's had a shock, Samuel. She'll be alright," the woman said.

"Good. Here we are, home again," he said.

Reining in my emotions, I asked, "Please, may I know your names?"

"I'm Clara and our driver is my husband, Samuel Witherspoon. Welcome to our home. What is your name?"

I had to think. "Oh, my name is...," I paused, trying to remember it. "Oh, yes, my name is Emeline. Emeline O'Connor."

The horse and cart had stopped. Samuel reached over the side of the cart and lifted me up in his strong arms. I winced with pain.

"I'll open the door, Samuel." Clara had stepped out of the cart and was headed up the path to a beautiful porch with an elaborate wood railing.

She opened the oak door, also decorative, and we entered the house. Samuel placed me on a single bed in a small room off what I supposed was a parlor or greeting area. "Oh," I said, my head pounding. "Thank you, Mr. Witherspoon."

"You're welcome. I'll be back after I take care of things outside."

Clara drew up a chair by my bedside. On her lap she held a box with antiseptic and medications in it. She also had a soft cloth, a sponge, some clean water in a pan, and strips of cloth bandages. "I don't know exactly what happened to you, but from the looks of it, someone tried to strangle you and your head must have hit a rock or something. There are bruises on your neck and a nasty gash on your forehead. Do you remember anything, Emeline O'Connor?"

"I'm traveling to Boston and I was just getting ready to go to bed in my tent. My horse, Dakota, made some noise and I went to investigate. Two men were there. I asked them to leave, but they wouldn't. The last thing I remember was that the taller of the two hid behind Dakota to shield himself from view and then lunged over to me and grabbed my neck." Then I shared the miracle of my visit to heaven with her.

"Oh, my goodness!" Clara took off the soiled bandages and wiped my forehead with an antiseptic soap and a sponge. "You might have been killed! It sounds like you had a peek at heaven." She patted the wound with a soft towel, put something greasy called Vaseline on it, and taped a cloth bandage over the top. "There now, that cut should heal nicely."

"Thank you, Mrs. Witherspoon."

"You're welcome. You get some rest now. I'll check on you in the morning. Good night, Emeline."

"Good night."

The feather pillow was soft under my head and the down coverlet wrapped around my body keeping me toasty warm. My head ached, but it didn't hurt as badly as it had last night. The smell of roasted coffee beans wafted over me as I took in my surroundings. My room was simply furnished: a single bed; a chair; a small table in the corner with a bowl, washcloth, towel and a pitcher of water;

and a rack with hooks on the back of the door. What I did notice was the woodwork around the doors and windows. They were surrounded by wide grooved planks of honey-colored wood, which had grooves on them, and in the corners were beautiful, ornate carved pieces.

"Good morning, Emeline. Did you sleep well?" Clara came in with a change of clothes for me. "I found this dress in your pack. Would you like to wear it today?" It was my rosebud dress with the sage sash! I remembered the last time I wore it I was with Miss Ambrose.

"Yes, ma'am, thank you."

"Are you able to change or will you need help?" She also gave me my bag with my hairbrush and ties, soap, toothbrush, and toothpaste.

"I can manage."

"Good. Come on out when you're ready." She smiled and closed the door behind her.

I took advantage of this opportunity to brush my teeth and wash myself, except for my hair which didn't need it yet. As I gingerly brushed my hair, I was careful not to hit my forehead or push too hard. Then I dressed. I smoothed the gathers on my skirt, tied the sash around my waist, and pulled my hair back with the matching hair scarf. I laid my soiled clothes in a pile behind the door, and came into the separate kitchen and dining area.

"Good morning, Emeline," said Samuel. "How are you feeling today?"

"So much better, thank you. I slept like a rock in that comfy bed." I took my seat across from him at the heavy trestle table. It was already set with white plates, flatware, and red cloth napkins.

"Emeline, would you like a cup of coffee?"

"I usually drink water or tea, but I'll try some. It smells delicious."

"Here you go." She set a cup of coffee on a saucer in front of me.

I took a sip. "Mmm. Such full flavor, it tastes good. I like it."

Clara was frying a mix of diced potatoes, onion, and bacon. The room was full of good smells.

"I put all of your belongings in the parlor last night. After breakfast, we'll take inventory," Samuel said.

I nodded and smiled, wrapping my hands around the warm coffee cup, my eyes meeting his.

"Here we are." Clara brought over two bowls for us: one with the potatoes and the other with scrambled eggs. She refilled our cups and took her place at the table.

"Thank you Clara," Samuel said as he passed around the food. Once we all had filled our plates, he prayed.

*"Dear God, thank you for all you have done, are doing,
and will do in our lives. And, thank you for leading us to
Emeline. We pray for the speedy healing of her wounds.
Bless this good food to our nourishment. Amen."*

"Amen," I said. The food tasted *so* good. "This breakfast is amazing, Mrs. Witherspoon. I thank you." When we had finished eating, I helped her clean up before we went into the parlor.

There on the floor was everything I had packed with me with one exception. "They took the money from my rucksack: the better part of twenty dollars and all the coin I had! But, everything else seems to be here. And my horse is here. Did they take his saddle?"

"No. I put it in the barn with your horse. He's enjoying hay and oats with ours."

"That's good. I'm surprised they didn't take Dakota and the saddle too." I didn't say anything yet about my money belt, which I was still wearing. *I'll have to figure how long that money will last.* "Thank you for taking care of Dakota."

"Surely. Happy to do it. We'd love for you to stay awhile, till you're ready to leave. Will you share your story with us? We'd like to know more about how you came to be here."

"It's a long story. Shall we sit?"

Samuel filled a cushioned armchair while Clara rocked her rocking chair. I sat on a cushioned stool they called an ottoman. I shared all that had happened since Pa's death, which took some time. Afterward, I asked, "You have a beautiful home. How did *you* come to be here?"

Samuel began, "My grandparents came from Scotland to America a long time ago. They were skilled woodworkers, and I continue doing their work today."

Clara said, "Samuel is very well-known in Indianapolis for his decorative wood trim. His work is found around the doors and windows, balusters for railings, fancy wooden staircases, custom lathed posts, and gingerbread trim for porches, gables, and the like."

"Boy! That's impressive. What a thrill to continue in your family's tradition."

"I do enjoy it and take a great deal of pride in my work. And we make a good living doing it. With all the hardwood lumber in Indiana, its a perfect location. Anyway, I met Clara, here, at a fall festival dance about ten years ago."

"We fell in love immediately," she laughed. "And we were married the next year."

I didn't see any children, so I thought it best not to ask about that. "That's nice."

"Would you like a tour of the shop?" Samuel asked.

"Really? Yes, please."

We walked out onto the porch, down a couple of steps, and over to a huge barn-like building. Stacks of hardwood boards and smaller sticks were at one end inside the building. It smelled of oak and maple; warm and lovely.

"This is my workbench where I design decorative gingerbread trimmings. Also, I do flatwork carving and special molding." Under the workbench was a large wooden box with several drawers. He opened them. "These are my chisels and knives; all different sizes. I have another case like this next to the lathe."

"You have quite a lot of them," I said. "They look very sharp."

"They have to be." Pointing to another shelf, he said, "Then there's my plane to make the wood even and smooth. Some planes are specially made for different styles of molding. Next to it is my adjustable ruler, square, and level. They're indispensable for trueing up the lumber." He picked up a tool with two arms with points on the ends and spread them apart and back together again. "This is a compass. I can measure angles and make circles with this. For bigger circles, I have this scribe tool."

"I was wondering how those circles were so perfect. I saw them in the corners of the trim in your house."

He held up another tool with a funny shape. "This is a drill bit auger for drilling holes. And, of course I have plenty of saws." He pointed to them hanging on one wall. "I love working with all of these hand tools, but this is my newest machine. It's called a wood lathe. See, it has three different speeds; you simply change the belt from the small to the medium or large wheel. The large wheel is the slowest. The stick of wood goes between these two points and is held fast."

"Could you show me how it works?"

"Sure." He pulled up a stool, placed his right foot on the peddle underneath and the stick of wood turned. He placed a chisel on the wood in a spot as it turned. The wood came off all around! As he moved it in and out, and up and down the length, he created a beautifully shaped piece. "It takes a steady hand and a plan to be able to repeat the same design over and again."

"Fascinating! It's no wonder you love doing this. You're quite the artisan." One more tool stood in the corner near the back door of the shop. It had two huge wheels and a little saw blade between them. A metal table was in the center. "What is that?"

"Oh, I almost forgot, that is my band saw. I use it to cut out the gingerbread pieces."

"I'd love to watch you do that sometime."

"Yes, if you're still here when I get my next order, you certainly may. Let's get back to the house. Clara will be looking for you."

Clara was watching us from the front porch. As she saw us coming, she asked, "How did you like the shop, Emeline?"

"It was wonderful." I smiled and looked at Samuel. "I hope you know how talented your husband is."

She smiled. "Yes, I know. Let's you and I chat while Mr. Witherspoon gets some work done today. He's got to finish an order of balusters before Monday. It's a good thing he has an apprentice, Jonathan. He'll be over later today."

"Call me when supper's ready, Clara," Samuel said as he strode back to the shop.

"I will. Be careful, Samuel."

"Is this Wednesday?" I had lost track of time.

"Yes, it is," Clara said.

"I need to do my devotional. Do you mind?"

"Not at all."

I lifted my rucksack up from the parlor floor and ambled into the small room. I opened the Bible to Matthew 5:8.

"Blessed are the pure in heart: for they shall see God."

I wrote:

Wednesday, March 26, 1890

"Dear Heavenly Father, I think I visited heaven last night. I want to be moral, upright, and pure in my life and someday come back to You. Thank you for letting me experience Your love. I love you, too. Amen."

I closed my journal and Bible and looked for Clara. She was in the kitchen now, peeling potatoes and carrots. "May I help?"

"Yes, have a seat. I'll get you another peeler."

We chatted as we peeled. A whole chicken with onions was braising on the stove and filled the air with its aroma. I was grateful that this loving couple had found me and taken care of me.

The next morning, I woke and read Matthew 5:9.

"Blessed are the peacemakers: for they shall
be called the children of God."

I wrote:

Thursday, March 27, 1890
"Thank you, Lord, for all you do for us. Bless the Witherspoons and let me be a blessing to them. Amen."

After my morning routine of washing, I found a pretty olive green calico dress, a deep yellow scarf, and a matching yellow sash hanging on the back of the door for me. It had a note pinned to it: '*Let's wash up your clothes today.*' Clara must have put that there. Even though it was a little loose, the sash gathered it around me nicely. "How kind!" There were even pockets in the side seams. I put a quarter in one of them from my money belt.

It was after seven o'clock and Samuel was already in the shop. The medicine box sat on the table next to some scissors and cotton balls. "Good morning, Emeline. That dress looks pretty on you. Let's change that dressing first." She pulled off yesterday's dressing, which didn't stick because of the vaseline, and cleaned it off again. "Actually, you're healing pretty quickly. I think one more day with a bandage and then we can leave it open to the air tomorrow. How do you feel today?"

"I feel fine. No more headache. Thank you for everything. I love this dress; the green goes with my hazel eyes."

"The yellow really sets off your dark brown hair too. Would you like some breakfast? We've already eaten, but I can fix you some oatmeal if you like."

"Oatmeal would hit the spot. Thank you."

As I ate the prepared hot cereal, we talked over immediate and future plans.

"So, Emeline, let's chat about your plans."

"As soon as my head heals, I must continue on to Boston, although I'm becoming quite nervous about riding Dakota the whole way alone after what happened. It seems the farther east I go the more people there are."

"Yes, and it will become quite crowded in some places, you'll find. Especially in big cities like Philadelphia, New York, and Boston."

"I've lost over half of the money I started out with. And, I've spent some too. I don't expect I should need much more than what I have if I just ride Dakota, but..."

"Have you thought of riding the train?"

"What would I do with Dakota? Could he go with me?"

"He could, I suppose, on the right train, but it would cost more. Dakota could stay here with us until you can send for him."

"That's a good idea. But how much is the train?"

"I don't rightly know, but we can find out at the station in Indianapolis."

"I'd still be alone on the train. How safe is it?"

"Pretty safe, most likely, but anything can happen anywhere in this world. It must be safer than traveling alone. Maybe you could send a letter to your grandfather and he could come here to ride with you?"

"I haven't written to anyone since I left! I promised Miss Ambrose and Ole Mr. Thompson I would too. And, I haven't written to my grandfather. I don't know his address."

"He doesn't even know you're coming?"

"No. He actually has never met me. Pa told me to take his gun for proof of who I am. You see there were initials carved... Oh, no! I don't remember seeing his gun in my belongings in the parlor." I scrambled to my feet and ran to the parlor to check. "No gun."

Sensing panic, Clara asked, "Do you have anything else of your Pa's?"

"Yes, I have his knife and Bible."

"Look in the front of the Bible. People often put their family tree information there."

I hurried to the bedroom and opened the Bible to the first pages. "Yes! There is my name. And, there are the names of my parents, his parents and grandparents, and Ma's parents and grandparents too."

"Perfect. Then the Bible will be your proof."

Relieved, I said, "May we take the cart into Indianapolis? I need to check the price of a train ticket and get a few two-cent postcards."

"We can check with the library to see if they have any references for people living in Boston."

"Yes. I have no idea where my grandfather lives – or even the name of his lithography company. All I know is his name: Silas O'Connor."

"Alright, let's get the horse and cart ready." She moved the pot of chicken to the side of the stove. "This will hold warm until we return."

"I can help, Mrs. Witherspoon! Show me the tack room." The horse barn had a separate tack room where bridles and bits hung on the wall, saddles straddled narrow benches, and a few blankets were stacked on a table. Currycombs and other necessities lay on a shelf. Next to Dakota, was a handsome chestnut quarter horse with a flaxen mane and tail and a white blaze down the front of his face. "He's gorgeous! What's your horse's name?"

Clara picked a bridle and approached the horse, letting him know she was there by touching his flank, and I picked up the top saddle blanket and followed. "His name is Applejack. He utterly adores apples."

"So does Dakota."

Once Applejack was hitched to the buggy, we were on our way. When we arrived in town, our first stop was the train station. Arched windows graced all the walls and the train's tracks ran right through the middle of the station. Clara waited with the cart while I went inside. At the ticket counter, I asked, "How much is a one-way ticket to Boston?"

The ticket master answered, "For one person, first class is $100, second class is $70, and third class is $30."

"How long is the trip?" I asked.

"About one full twenty-four-hour day plus six hours, miss."

"Boy, that's fast!"

He smiled, "Yes, miss. Steam engines are changing the world. It would be faster if we didn't stop at several towns along the way for passengers and to fill up with water. When are you planning to go? We have a train leaving every day but Sunday."

"I'm not sure yet. Thank you for the pricing."

"You're welcome."

I shared the information with Clara. "So I'll need more money just for the train ride, and I probably will need some to live on until I locate my grandfather."

"We'll tell Mr. Witherspoon. Maybe you can help out in the shop and earn some money. I'm sure he'd love to help."

My eyes lit up at the prospect of working on the wood lathe. "Oh, I *do* hope so."

"Let's go to the library and ask if they have any records of people or businesses in Boston."

"Alright."

The library was even bigger than the train station. It had banks of rectangular windows all around the second story, and arched windows all around the main floor. There were even smaller windows for a basement level underground! Inside were tremendous darkly stained, wooden bookcases filled with books of all kinds. I advanced to the front desk. "Would you have any information about where people live in other cities, like Boston? Or, even businesses?"

"I'm sorry, miss. We have that kind of information for Indianapolis, but not other cities. Can I help with anything else?"

I noticed there were postcards for sale on the desk, each with a picture of the library on it. "I'd like five of those please."

"That will be ten cents."

I pulled a quarter from my side pocket and tucked away the change. "Thank you." I slipped the postcards in the other side pocket and tiptoed over to Clara who was browsing the titles in the fiction section.

"All set?"

"Yes, ma'am. I found the postcards here, but no information on where Grandfather Silas might live." We returned home to talk to Samuel.

That afternoon, we did my laundry and hung my clothes up to dry. Then we finished the supper of chicken, potatoes, and carrots. We each enjoyed a healthy portion, which included a chunk of wheat bread.

In the evening, we sat in the parlor, visited about my plans, and discussed the possibility of my helping in the shop. Samuel was excited to give me a lesson the very next day!

I still had decisions to make. Thoughts swirled through my head as I lay in bed. Sleep eluded me. *Do I continue on to Boston alone on the train? Do I continue to Boston riding Dakota? Or, should I stay here with the Witherspoons? Or, return home? If I take the train to Boston, what will happen to Dakota? Will I ever see him again? I can't ask Pa; I have to decide for myself. What do I really want?*

Finding Funds

What do I really want? With so many options, it was difficult to know. I sought solace and direction in the Bible. I picked up where I left off; Matthew 5:10.

"Blessed are they which are persecuted for righteousness'
sake: for theirs is the kingdom of heaven."

It was after midnight, so I wrote:

Friday, March 28, 1890
"Yesterday I spent time with the Witherspoons. Thank you for sending them to rescue me, Lord. They have given me so much. I am confused about my mission. Help me to make the right decision; the one that's best for me."

I slept.

Clara came into the bedroom and woke me around eight o'clock in the morning with another attractive dress and apron to wear, as well as the medicine box. "Mr. Witherspoon is in the shop with Jonathan finishing up the order that's due Monday." She hung the dress on the hook behind the door. "He said to send you out around eleven o'clock. That gives you time to get cleaned up and ready for the day, have breakfast, and write your postcards. The postman usually comes around two o'clock."

"Thank you, Mrs. Witherspoon," I said, sitting up and wiping my eyes on my shirtsleeve.

She came over to the bed and sat down beside me. "Let's see how your forehead is healing."

The air felt cool to the wound when the bandage was removed. Clara used a soft, soapy cloth and dabbed it on the cut to disinfect it once more. "I would say you could go without it now, but because you'll be in the shop today, we'd better go one more day with a bandage."

"Good idea." I sat still, watching her as she gently attended to my wound. "What can you tell me about Jonathan?"

"Oh, he's a young man, maybe three years older than you. He wants to get into the woodworking business, so Samuel is teaching him. He's gained quite a lot of skill over the past year and shows great promise. He keeps to his schedule and has been a real help as our business has grown. He earns a fair wage too.

"That is a very pretty dress. Blue is my favorite color. Is it one of yours?"

"Yes. I thought this one would compliment your eyes. There. You're all set. I'll see you later at the table." Clara packed her box and closed the door behind her.

I sighed. Clara and Ma had a lot in common. After washing and brushing my teeth, I slipped on the sky blue dress with tiny white dots all over it. A bright, white scarf was with it to tie my hair back. Over it, I put on the white apron and tied it behind me.

At the table, Clara said, "Oh, Emeline, that blue dress does become you." Breakfast was simple: apple quarters, sliced cheddar cheese, scrambled eggs, and a small glass of milk.

"Thank you." I noticed she had already put the inkwell and quill with my postcards on the table. "So much has happened. I couldn't fit everything on one little postcard." I turned the first one over.

Clara laughed. "True. Short and sweet, as they say."

"Hmm. I'll address them first. Mr. Pickwick will deliver Mr. Thompson's."

Miss Ambrose, c/o The Schoolhouse, Kearney, MO
Mr. Thompson, c/o The Mercantile, Kearney, MO
Mr. Pickwick, c/o The Mercantile, Kearney, MO
Mr. & Mrs. Cooper, 25 E. Washington St., Kearney, MO
Harriet Hudson, 26 E. Washington St., Kearney, MO

I wrote on each, in my best and smallest handwriting, that after a tumultuous trip, I had arrived safely in Indianapolis. I would continue on to Boston by train. I had decided that Dakota would stay with new friends in Indianapolis until I could send for him. I added a personal line for each person and then I signed, "I miss you, Emeline."

There it was: my decision. I was being true, not only to Pa, but to myself. *I really want to meet my grandfather and be with true family again. Not just for Pa, but for myself. And, I can always do something else after I've met Grandfather Silas if I want to.* "Now then. They're ready to go." I gathered them together.

"That's fine," Mrs. Witherspoon said with a grin. "It's nearly eleven. Go ahead and put them in the postbox by the road and go on over to the woodworking shop; I'll drop in later. I need to catch up on my mending."

As I crunched across the gravel path, I could hear noises coming from the workshop: a regular click, an intermittent whir, and a rhythmic swoosh. The door was propped open. I entered and found Samuel standing at the wood lathe, pumping the treadle underneath, and skillfully carving a piece of maple into an ornate spindle. A handsome young man worked at the bench on another piece of wider maple. He was carving hills and valleys into its flat face with a special plane to create a decorative molding. I stood near Samuel and watched him work. "That looks like loads of fun, but difficult."

He laughed. "Just about finished with this one." He picked up some wood shavings and held them onto the piece as it turned, rubbing it from one end to the other. "See how a pile of shavings takes off all the little scratches and burs? It almost shines now." He took the spindle off the machine and handed it to me.

"It's so smooth. Someday, I'd like to try."

"First, we'll start you on sharpening our chisels. As you work, you can practice with them on scrap pieces of wood. Your chance on the wood lathe will come if there's enough time before you leave." He turned toward the workbench. "Jon, here's someone I'd like you to meet."

The young man stopped and turned toward me, wiping his hands on his canvas apron. His dark brown hair curled loosely over his forehead and contrasted with his blue eyes. His smile was dazzling. "How do you do," he said. "My name is Jonathan."

I stammered, "Um. Hello. My name is Emeline." My cheeks grew hot.

"Samuel told me about you. How long do you think you'll stay?"

"Just until I earn enough to buy a train ticket to Boston. I'm not sure yet."

"Well, it's nice to meet you. I'd better get back to work now. Perhaps we can visit later." He winked at me and looked at Samuel.

"Thank you," I said, my voice lilting up as if it were a question.

"Come over here and I'll show you how to sharpen tools, Emeline," Samuel said with a grin.

Grateful for the task, I gave him my full attention. I was standing in front of a table with a vise and a board with three flat black stones. "What are these?"

"These are sharpening stones. Let me show you." He was holding a flat chisel, which was about one-half inch wide. "See this bevel?

That's what we're going to sharpen. It's important that you hold it exactly at the angle of the bevel. We don't want to lose that. We just need the edge sharpened. To succeed at this kind of woodcraft, you need patience, practice, hardwoods like maple, oak, cherry, or walnut, and good, sharp hand tools. If you sat down at the lathe with a piece of pine and a chisel, it would gum up with the sap from the soft wood and be rough-looking. Even with a piece of good hardwood, if your chisels are dull, your cuts will be rough and not precise. So, this is a very important job."

"I see. I'll do my best."

He put a little water on each of the three stones. "Now. You hold the chisel so the bevel is flat against the first stone, the coarse grit, and rub it away from you and then back to you. Not side-to-side. Do that about thirty times. Then move to the next stone, which is a medium grit, and repeat. Finally, do the same on the last stone, the finest grit. Let me show you."

He put a piece of scrap wood into the vice and used an unsharpened chisel on it. "Hold it against the wood like this and push to the left." A shaving came off. "See how rough the wood is after this cut?" Then he went through the sharpening procedure and cut the wood again. "Now, feel this cut."

"It's smooth!"

"Right. A sharp tool makes all the difference. Now, you try it."

I took another dull chisel and scraped the wood. "It seems sharp to me. It cut the wood, but I see it isn't smooth."

"Uh-huh," he said, hands in his pockets.

It took awhile, but I sharpened this chisel on all three stones, and then cut again. "Oh, that was much easier and smoother."

"Right, then. You've got it. I'll leave you to it and go back to the lathe. Just ask if you have any questions, and *be careful.* I don't want you to cut yourself!"

"I will."

About three hours later, I was finished with the sharpening task. "I'm finished, Mr. Witherspoon," I said. "May I do anything else?"

"There's a broom and dustpan next to the barrel of shavings in the corner. You can sweep up for us."

"Alright." I grabbed the broom and swept the whole shop, excusing myself when I got close to Jonathan and Samuel. They both politely moved away so I could sweep, and returned.

"That's good," said Samuel. "I think we're finished for the day. "I hear Mrs. Witherspoon coming."

Clara came into the shop with a basket of eggs over her arm. "Look what the hens gave us today: eight lovely brown eggs. How did you like working in the wood shop today, Emeline?"

"It's wonderful! I learned to sharpen chisels today. I'm so impressed with the beauty of this work."

"We have been receiving lots of new orders. More and more people are moving here and building houses, and they love to put this fancy woodwork in them." Turning to Samuel and Jonathan, she asked. "How did it go today?"

"Very well. We are on schedule to deliver the balusters and molding Monday afternoon," Samuel said.

"See this?" With a broad smile, Jonathan showed Clara a piece of the molding he'd finished. "I love the smoothness of all the peaks and valleys."

Clara ran her hand over the work. "That is excellent workmanship, Jonathan. You should be proud."

"Thank you. Well, shall I see you all Monday morning, bright and early, about 7:00?" Jonathan asked.

"Sounds good. See you then. Have a nice weekend, Jon," said Samuel.

"Goodbye!" He saw me smile and wave before he turned to walk away.

Oh, my heart.

Samuel locked the doors after we left the shop and headed toward the house. Inside, we sat in the parlor for awhile, talking about the day and the plans for the next. For the Witherspoons, Saturday was set aside as a day for doing laundry and working around the house.

Specifically, tomorrow was a day for planting the vegetable garden and I was invited. Samuel and Applejack would plow the furrows, while Clara and I planted and covered seeds of bush string beans, carrots, radishes, peas, and broccoli. Inside the house, she had a box of dirt for seeding tomatoes. Because nights could still be cold, the tomato seedlings would be transplanted later to the garden.

"May I ride Dakota for awhile after the garden is planted? I miss riding him." It had been days since we arrived.

"Surely," Samuel said. "In fact, I forgot to tell you. I've let him into our fenced pasture for the last two days. He's been enjoying the grass, romping around with Applejack, and having a grand time.

And, so, life went on with the Witherspoons for about a month. I had
written more postcards home, continued my Bible reading and prayers,
watched the garden grow, and had learned more about woodworking,
and Jonathan.

I've got to admit that Jonathan was not making it easier for me to leave.
He was always kind and friendly, but not too much. I mean, we were just
friends. After all, I am only thirteen years old. Too young for anything more
than that. But, during work, we talked about things we liked or didn't like.
Things that were important to us. We shared memories of special times and
people. He joked with me because, he said, he liked my laugh.

Samuel let him teach me how to use the plane and make molding
trim. I even sharpened the blade for the plane. At last, Samuel said
it was time for me to try my hand at the wood lathe. I had watched
him often and had learned a lot just by watching.

"You've watched. Now, you'll do. It's a skill that takes a lot of
practice - especially if you have to do things exactly the same way
multiple times. Don't expect this first piece to be anything at all.
I want you to just play with the tools this time. Get a feel for how
they work. Don't worry about style, measurements, or anything. Try
different kinds of chisels as you go."

"Great!" I got into position in front of the lathe, which was bolted
to the floor. The belt was on the largest top wheel, which meant the
slowest speed. "Is this the correct wheel?"

"For now, yes. Now, hold the chisel with both hands, as you've seen me do. Move the block to steady your hands when you need to. Use whichever foot you want on the treadle and start it up." The now familiar whirring started. "Just touch the wood with the corner of your chisel and ease it into the wood." The wood shavings came off with sort of a vibrating sound.

"I'm doing it!" I tried going deeper, tried making a round shape by going right and left along the length of the wood. I turned the chisel the other direction, holding my hands the opposite way and tried to make a convex curve. It was amazing how differently each chisel carved the wood. Some chisels were flat, some were curved, and another had a deep "V" shape. "This is so much fun!"

Samuel laughed, "Yes, I enjoy it too, very much. It never gets old for me. Each piece is unique – even if it ends up looking exactly like another – because each piece of wood is unique." He changed out the wood for a new piece of maple for me. "You just keep changing these and practice. Make sure you get it locked in tight." He pulled at the lever. "Once you think you have it tight, make it turn for a moment, then stop, and tighten it again. Tomorrow, I'll show you how I made this spindle." He set one down near the machine.

I discovered I loved woodworking. For the next two weeks, I made spindles. The first were of marginal quality, at best. But each day I showed improvement until they were nearly as good as Samuel's. He just had to spend a minute or two to perfect them.

One evening after supper, I announced, "It's taken longer than I anticipated, but I have enough money now to continue my journey."

"I'm doing it!" I tried going deeper, tried making a round shape by going left and right along the length of the wood

Clara set down her embroidery in her lap. Samuel closed his book and put his fingertips together, his elbows on the arms of the chair. Clara said, "We knew this day would come." She wiped the corner of her eye with the cuff of her sleeve.

"We all have grown very attached to you, Emeline," Samuel said. "I know you'll keep in touch and let us know how you're doing." He leaned forward, elbows on his knees, his chin resting on his hands, fingers locked together. "If you ever want to come back and stay with us, we'd welcome you with open arms. Consider us family, Emeline."

"Oh, my!" I wasn't expecting this to be so hard. "I would be honored."

Samuel relaxed back into his chair and rocked. "We'll miss you."

"I will miss you too. I would love to stay right now, but I really want to get to know my grandfather before it's too late. I hope you can understand that."

"We do. When do you want to leave?" Clara pulled the train schedule out of a book in the bookcase. "It looks like there's a train leaving at 8:00 in the morning on Friday. That gives you a day to get ready. And you'll want to say good-bye to Jonathan and Dakota."

"Friday is perfect. And it's early enough that my departure won't interfere with the day's work here." I said. "Do I need to purchase the ticket early?"

"Yes. We should go to the train station tomorrow," Clara replied.

That night in bed, I opened the Bible to Matthew 5 again. I had been reading the book of John during my stay, but now I wanted to return to the Beatitudes. I read Matthew 5:11 and 12.

11 *"Blessed are ye, when men shall revile you, and persecute you,*
and shall say all manner of evil against you falsely, for my sake."

12 *"Rejoice and be exceeding glad for great is*
your reward in heaven: for so persecuted they
the prophets which were before you."

I wrote:

Wednesday, May 7, 1890

"Dear Father in heaven, thank you for your protection and provision on this journey. I ask You for safe travel and that my search for my grandfather be a quick one. Bless my grandfather and friends, both old and new. Amen."

Thursday morning, after breakfast, Clara and I took the buggy to the station. The now familiar building with its arched windows and doors held a new excitement for me. "I've never ridden a train before."

"I have, a long time ago. When I rode it there was just one passenger car and one ticket price. Now they have the plain, medium, and fancy cars," she said.

"Plain is fine for me." We approached the ticket master's counter. "I'd like to purchase a one-way, third-class ticket to Boston, please, for the eight o'clock train on Friday."

"Very well. That will be $30, miss," he said. He looked very official in his suit with braided trim and conductor hat. His handlebar mustache was thick and waxed so that it turned up at the ends.

I pulled out cash I had packed in my pocket and gave it to him. "Here you are."

He began counting all the dollars and coins, of which there were considerable. "Just checking. Yes, it's all there. Thank you, miss. Here is your ticket. Don't lose it, now! We'll see you Friday morning. Be here about a half hour before departure."

"Pardon me," Mrs. Witherspoon said. "Would there be a railroad employee, maybe a conductor, whom I could speak with on Friday morning?"

"Yes, ma'am. There will be three conductors, one for each car. You can speak to the third class conductor who will be helping people board."

"Thank you, sir," she said. We turned around and headed back for the buggy.

"Ah well, that's done," I said.

Mrs. Witherspoon gave me a weak smile, but her eyes flickered on and off my face. "Tch, Tch," she said to Applejack. The rest of that day was awkwardly silent. First, I washed all my soiled clothing and hung it out to dry. Clara was kind enough to give me the two dresses I had been wearing. "You'll need more than one dress in Boston," she said. That makes three dresses, plus my two riding outfits, coat, hat, and boots that I own. I made a list of things to pack in my rucksack for the trip. I wouldn't need everything I came with at first. I would wear my money belt with most of my money in it, and I pinned the pocket watch inside my dress pocket. Since the train stopped for twenty minutes to refill, I would need to know the time!

At the end of the afternoon, it was time for a teary good-bye to Jonathan and Dakota. Jonathan gave me a big bear hug and told me to write. Dakota had no idea why I was crying as my arms circled his neck. He snorted and pawed the ground.

That night, I packed my rucksack, maybe for the last time. I read Matthew 5:13.

"Ye are the salt of the earth: but if the salt have lost his savor, wherewith shall it be salted? It is thenceforth good for nothing, but to be cast out, and to be trodden under foot of men."

I thought about that. What is it to be salt? Then I thought about the properties of salt: it preserves, it cleanses, it causes thirst.

I wrote:

Thursday, May 8, 1890

"Dear Lord, I think I understand. You want us to preserve your Word, to clean up evil in the world, and to draw other people to You. Help me to be salt in Boston, and even on this train ride. Thank you. Amen."

"This is harder than I imagined," I said to Clara Friday morning as I put on my rucksack after an early breakfast.

"It's difficult for us too. We will miss you, Emeline." Clara held my hands and kissed my cheek. "Godspeed."

"Time to go," Samuel said. We all walked to the buggy and Samuel helped Clara and me get in. Three on the buggy seat was snug, but doable. "Tch, Tch," he clicked to Applejack.

At the station, we pulled into a space and tied Applejack to a rail. The three of us went into the station's arched doorway and stared at the huge train that went right through the center of the room. Its engine was huffing outside as men filled it with water for the steam and wood for the fire. There were three cars, but all of them were third class this trip. I was directed to the first car behind the engine. The conductor was helping people up the stairs and into their seats, taking their tickets as he did so.

Clara sought the conductor and said, "Sir, would you do us a great favor and watch after this young lady on the trip. She is traveling alone. Just check on her now and then and make sure no harm comes to her, would you please?"

The gentleman smiled and nodded. "I'd be happy to. Don't worry about the lass. I won't let anything bad happen."

"Thank you," Clara said. She turned and hugged me tightly. Then she took my arms and looked directly into my eyes. "You be careful, Emeline, and be sure to write as soon as you can when you get there. We'll be watching the postbox every day. Here's a bag of food for your trip." She handed me a paper bag.

I kissed her cheek. "Thank you, Mrs. Witherspoon."

Samuel gave me a big hug too. "Farewell, Emeline O'Connor. We'll take good care of Dakota. Come back and see us."

"I will," I said, kissing his cheek, too. "And, thank you for teaching me about wood carving."

I handed over my ticket and climbed the three steps into the railway car. Inside were rows of wooden bench seats with a narrow aisle between them. Two people sat on each side of the car on each row. In the back, there was a community "washroom." There might have been ten rows, I didn't count them, but I found an open seat by a window, which was opened for fresh air. I removed my rucksack from my back, placed it under my feet, and sat down.

After a few more minutes, I heard the train bell. Ding, ding. ding, ding. Ding, ding. A long, low whistle followed: toooot, toot, toot, toooot. Then I heard a chuffing sound as the steam started pushing and the wheels squealed, grinding against the metal rails. I smiled and waved to the Witherspoons and they waved back. The chuffing got faster and faster. The squealing stopped, except for around curves. I watched the countryside go by in a flash. I was *finally* on my way again!

Riding the Rails

Just think, I would be asleep somewhere in Boston tomorrow night! For at least an hour, I sat glued to the window, watching the countryside pass. Occasionally, I could see the engine at the front of the train as we curved left. The chuffing made clouds of steam rise from the tall stack at the front of the engine — a contrast of white against a clear blue sky. Beautiful!

The ride was fairly smooth, much smoother than riding horseback. It did vibrate and sway side-to-side sometimes. I could continuously hear the chuffing of the engine, but the engineer also rang the bell and blew the horn whenever there was someone in the way or if we were approaching a small town. We stopped at nearly every one.

I turned around and looked at the other passengers. Since it was third class, most of the people wore plain clothes in varying degrees of cleanliness. Some people traveled alone while others were couples. There were a few families with babies and small children who were very loud at first, but quieted down with the noise and motion of the car. A man traveling alone was seated next to me. He wore dark gray slacks, a white shirt, and a gray pin-striped vest. His dark hair was neatly trimmed as were his mustache and beard.

"Hello. My name is Emeline O'Connor," I said, offering a friendly smile.

He turned toward me and returned a smile. "Hello, Emeline. My name is Mr. McCarthy. What brings you this way?"

"I'm meeting my grandfather in Boston," I said. "How about you?"

"I'm helping the YMCA."

"What is the YMCA?"

"It's short for Young Men's Christian Association. They do many things, but I'm helping spread the word about summer camps. We want to provide a positive place for children to make new friends, build confidence, and gain self-reliance."

"What a great mission." I shifted my body toward him for better eye contact. His eyes were as gray as clouds on a stormy day, but kind. "Does the YMCA have a place for people to live temporarily in Boston? I need a place to stay when I arrive as I don't yet know where my grandfather lives."

"No, not with the YMCA, but you might stay at our boarding house. Mrs. McCarthy takes care of it while I'm out of town. It is our home, but we have divided some of the rooms up into smaller ones to rent out to people we know or have been recommended to us."

"Ooh. That sounds perfect." I hesitated. His speech was so different from mine; much like Pa's. "But, how much will it cost?"

"We have one room available now. Rent is $8.00 per month and board is $3.75 per week. The food is wholesome and good."

Just think, I would be asleep somewhere in Boston tomorrow night!

"It sounds perfect for me. One month should be more than enough time. May I ride with you from the train station as well? I can pay you."

"Sure. Mrs. McCarthy will meet us there with the carriage."

"Thank you, Mr. McCarthy." Satisfied that all was going well, I stood up, picked up my rucksack, and set it on the seat. I retrieved my Bible, journal, and pencil, and then set the rucksack back on the floor.

"Read the Bible, do you?" Mr. McCarthy asked.

"Yes. And I keep a journal."

He lit a pipe and puffed on it to get it started and then took out a small Bible from an inside pocket of his vest to read. The pipe tobacco smelled sweet, like cookies.

In mine I read Matthew 5:14-16

14 *"Ye are the light of the world. A city that is set on an hill cannot be hid."*

15 *"Neither do men light a candle, and put it under a bushel, but on a candlestick; and it giveth light unto all that are in the house."*

16 *"Let your light so shine before men, that they may see your good works, and glorify your Father which is in heaven."*

Friday, May 9, 1890

Dear Heavenly Father, here I am. Make me a light to glorify you that others will see and be moved by. Thank you for everything, especially for always being there for me — and everyone.

The train lumbered on, stopping every so often to let people on or off. Our little car's passengers were always changing. But, Mr. McCarthy would go all the way to Boston. When we got off at big cities, I grabbed my rucksack and walked around the train yard with him. Once, we went inside the depot to eat and I set my rucksack down beside me. It fell off the bench and some things fell out, but I stuffed them back in.

Sometimes we walked up to the big engine and just looked at its gleaming appointments: bell, whistle, colorful paint. Back on the train, I would sleep now and then, leaning against the side of the moving passenger car for a few hours at a time, but it was hard to sleep.

After Indiana, we stopped in Columbus, Ohio. Then, Pittsburgh, Pennsylvania. Then Philadelphia, Pennsylvania. We cut across New Jersey, Connecticut, and Rhode Island, and then we were in New York, New York. Boston, Massachusetts was the next stop!

"Just think," I said to Mr. McCarthy as we walked around the New York station. "I have traveled through nine states already. Massachusetts will make ten!"

Smiling, he said, "That's a mighty long distance alright, Miss Emeline. Let's get back on board now, before it rains." Mr. McCarthy looked up at the low gray clouds hanging in the sky. "The air is heavy with humidity."

Settled in my seat once more, I was excited for the next, and last, stop for me. "I'm anxious to meet Mrs. McCarthy."

He lit his pipe again. "She is a wonderful person. You'll like her, and our daughter, Mallory."

"You have a daughter? How old is she?"

"She's twelve and will be excited to have you around."

"How fun! I miss my good friend Harriet." More seriously, I said, "But the most important thing I must do is find my grandfather. I think I'll read a little now."

I stood and set my rucksack on the wooden seat and felt for Pa's Bible, but I didn't feel it. Digging through the clothes and other things, my fingers explored everyplace. It wasn't there! "Mr. McCarthy, have you seen my Bible?"

"No, Emeline, I haven't. Not since yesterday actually. Is it missing?"

"Yes!"

"Let me help you look." He stood up with me and he searched the rucksack too. "Not here. Maybe it fell on the floor?"

"Maybe. Let's look around our seats."

"I don't see it."

"Let's ask if anyone else has." I approached the conductor and spoke to him softly.

The conductor stood at the front of the car and said, "Excuse me. Excuse me, please. May I have your attention? One of our passengers has lost her Bible. Has anyone seen one anywhere on the car? It's very important to her. Please stand and look around your seats."

Everyone cooperated and looked under and behind each seat and piece of baggage. They murmured, some shook their heads, and many held out their hands indicating, no, they didn't see it anywhere.

"Alright. Thank you for looking," the conductor said. To me, he said, "Sorry, miss, I don't believe it's on the train."

"I appreciate your efforts. Thank you," I said as I returned to my seat and stared out the window. Every now and then, I could see the ocean. We were so close to Boston now.

"Would you like to borrow my Bible to read?" asked Mr. McCarthy.

"Thank you. Maybe in a little while." Now I feared failure. I must stop and think. I wanted to write to Pa in my journal about my feelings. So, I opened my journal and wrote:

Saturday, May 10, 1890

Dear Pa, I think of you often and I know you must be enjoying heaven with Ma now. If you've been watching, you know how hard this trip has been for me, but I am still trying to get to Grandfather Silas and I'm looking forward to getting to know him for myself.

Pa, I'm not sure anymore about how this will go. First of all, I don't have your gun anymore. Remember, you said it would be my proof of who I am? Then, Mrs. Witherspoon showed me our family history in the front of your Bible and suggested it would work just as well. But now it's gone too.

I'm worried I will fail to find my grandfather in the first place. I've no idea where he is; and this is a big city. I'm worried that he won't believe me when I introduce myself. Or that, if he does, he won't be happy about my coming. You said, "Family is important." What if Grandfather throws that back at me with a comment like, "If he thought family was so important, why did he leave?" Finally, what if he isn't even alive anymore? ~ Love, Emeline

I closed my eyes and journal for a moment to think. Was this trip completely unnecessary and foolish? *No, I do want to learn about Grandfather Silas, the last blood relative I know I have.* I thought about the farm back at Kearney where life was simple. Chores, school, family, and friends. All that changed when Pa died. How easy it would have been to stay in Indianapolis with the Witherspoons, Dakota, and Jonathan. Am I getting ready to embark on another alternate reality by rooming with the McCarthys in Boston? I only have enough money for one month right now. I have so many unanswered questions. With no immediate solution, I must at least room with the McCarthys until I decide what to do, again. I sighed. I was confident things would work out, one way or another. One thing I had learned was that change is a certainty.

Outside there were lots of buildings coming up, some of them tall. The closer we came, the more buildings there were crowded together.

Streets were full of people, horse-drawn carts, and something else. "What's that, Mr. McCarthy?"

"Those are trolleys," he said. "Three horses usually pull them all around town. They have regular, scheduled routes they take. Some people ride them instead of driving their own carriages while they're in the city."

"Oh!" I'd never seen anything like this before, nor crowds of people such as this. "There are so many people."

He laughed. "Yaw, it's quite different from your home town in Missouri, and I'm sure it will be an adjustment for you, but I think you'll come to like it in Boston."

"I hope so."

We pulled into the Fitchburg train station and waited until we had come to a complete stop. I stood up and put on my rucksack. The conductor opened the door and we filed out, row by row, until all those terminating their trip in Boston were off. "Thank you," the conductor said.

"Thank you, and good-bye," I replied.

Mr. McCarthy led the way to the exit. "Impressive building, isn't it?"

"I'll say it is." There were two rails that went through the building: one for each direction, coming or going. Inside, the massive rock walls rose to an astonishing height. Once outside, I noticed it was more than two stories high and there were two huge, six-sided towers with stone faces that rose way above the top of the building. They resembled towers like you might see in old castles of Europe. "My, but this station is fancy."

Mr. McCarthy smiled. "Yaw, and it's been here a long, long time. There's my wife over there." He waved at her as she stood by their carriage.

Calling it a buggy would have been an understatement. The carriage had two seats: a front and a back. It was pulled by a lovely, albeit very stocky, bay horse. She had white stockings with long white hair that hung over her hooves and a white blaze on her face. Her mane and tail were nearly black. I walked alongside Mr. McCarthy as we crossed the street, which was busy with people walking, horses pulling carriages and carts, and people riding something with only two wheels. "What are those?"

"Oh, those are bicycles," he said.

I wondered how they stay up on two wheels. Boston was like another world.

"Hello, darling," he said as he grabbed his wife's hands and gave her a kiss. "I'd like you to meet Miss Emeline O'Connor, who I met on the train. She will be renting a room from us for a month. We do still have it, don't we?"

"Happy to meet you, Miss Emeline." She shook my right hand and turned to her husband. "Yaw, it is still vacant. Welcome." Her pretty peach and cream dress had a high neckline trimmed with ivory lace, lots of material gathered in the bodice, high puffed sleeves, and a bell-shaped skirt. On her head, she wore a fancy hat with color-coordinated ribbons.

"Thank you," I said.

"Let's go home now." Mr. McCarthy helped me up into the back seat of the carriage and then his wife up to the front. He climbed up and gathered the reins. "Home, Penny." The heavy horse had no trouble pulling us, while I took in the sights around me.

The street was covered with cobblestones so you could hear the clip-clop of the horses hooves everywhere: quite a din. It was a wide road, wide enough to allow a trolley through the middle, and other horse traffic going opposite directions on either side. It was so busy, that Penny followed the carriage in front of us closely, and someone else's horse was right behind us. The smell of dung permeated the air. "That's a strong smell," I said, as I waved a fly away from my face.

"Yaw. We have street cleaners that clean the streets every morning," said Mr. McCarthy.

The sidewalks were crowded with people who were mostly dressed in fine clothing. "I've never seen so many fancy hats on women before. And their dresses are so intricate. The men are mostly wearing suits, ties, and hats like I've not seen before."

Mrs. McCarthy said, "Yaw, you'll find Boston is up-to-date with the latest fashions and rules of etiquette."

"Etiquette?"

"Manners," she said. "There's even a book with all of the rules listed. I'll show you whenever you like."

"Thank you." I hoped the manners my parents taught me were good enough. Goodness!

The buildings in Boston were immense, massive, historic structures mostly made of brick or stone. Carvings adorned them as well as buttresses, which stuck out from some of the higher levels. Large, interesting signs hung above storefronts. A large clock sat precariously on top of a thick post. Train tracks wove through different parts of the city too.

There was so much city, you could barely see the sky, except for above your head. For that matter, there wasn't much grassy land either. Occasionally, there would be a park or just a small green space. It felt overpowering, claustrophobic. No wonder Pa wanted to leave for open spaces!

"Almost there," Mr. McCarthy said. "Once we turn on this next street, we'll be home."

Thankfully, the next street, Tremont, was less congested. It led to an area of homes. We turned from Tremont to Dover and plodded between blocks of tall, four-story homes made of brick. Some had an alcove of three sides in front of the building's front door. Some had little balconies above the front door with access to them from the second floor. The buildings were divided into separate houses only by the architectural details. Really, they were one massive building for the length of one block.

"We're home!" Mr. McCarthy announced as he pulled Penny over and stopped.

"Oh, my!" I said. Theirs was one of the homes with the balcony over the front door. Potted plants enjoyed the sun there: ferns, palms, and some beautiful red flowers. "What a lovely home."

"Thank you," said Mrs. McCarthy. Mr. McCarthy helped her down, and then me. We walked up seven steps to the front door and entered the home. "Let me show you to your room, Emeline."

Mr. McCarthy took Penny and the carriage somewhere down the street.

Silently, I followed her through the parlor and up the staircase to the second floor. We passed two women and a man before we reached my room, which had one window to a grassy courtyard between the houses. "It's lovely," I said. There was a small bed, nightstand, and small chest of drawers. Hooks on the back of the door provided a place for hanging clothes. A painting of a beach scene hung on a light gray wall. "Where do I wash up? I don't see a pitcher or bowl."

"I'll show you. Just set down your pack and follow me."

Next door was a large room with a white tile floor and tile halfway up the walls. There were white fixtures too. "What is this?"

"This is our guest bathroom. This is your sink." She turned a handle and water came out. "Hot or cold. The left is for hot water."

"Where does the water go?"

"Down the drain and into the sewer system. And, this is a bigger version of the same thing: the bathtub. You turn on the water with both handles, adjusting the temperature as you like, take off your clothes, and take a bath. The soap is in the dish." She pointed to a dish attached to the wall. "When you're finished, dry off with one of the huckaback towels from the shelves. Put on your robe, and return to your room to dress. Do you have a robe, Emeline? Or a nightgown?"

"No, ma'am."

"That's alright. We can loan you one until you can get another. I'll bring them up for you and hang them on the hook behind the door."

"Thank you. What's this?" I pointed to a thing that looked like a seat with a tall pipe that disappeared into another white box near the ceiling.

"That's the toilet. You haven't seen this before?"

"No."

"You don't have to go outside to relieve yourself anymore. Just raise the lid, have a seat, and do your business. When you're finished, use the toilet paper on that roll to clean yourself and drop it in the bowl too. Then, stand up, and flush."

"Flush?"

"Pull this chain handle. The water from up there will come down, flush away everything in the bowl, and refill it for the next use." She smiled at me. "It's quite an improvement from having to go outside, yaw?"

"I'll say it is. What about privacy?"

"When you use this room, close the door, press the little button on the doorknob and it will be locked. It will unlock when you turn it to leave. If the door is closed, always knock to make sure it's unoccupied. All the renters use the same bathroom, so we ask that you clean up after you use it in consideration for the next person. The cleaning supplies are in the cabinet under the sink. Any questions?"

"Not right now, thank you. May I settle into my room now? And, I can pay you for the month, and for the week of meals too."

"You can bring that down later. Why don't you unpack, clean up, and change your clothes."

"Oh, thank you. It's been nearly two days! What time shall I come down for supper?" I pulled out pa's pocket watch. It read four o'clock.

"Supper will be served promptly at six o'clock. But you can come down before that. I'll have Mallory give you a tour."

"Mallory! Where is she?"

"Visiting friends. She'll be home soon. I'm sure she'll be ecstatic to meet you." Mrs. McCarthy left and walked down the stairs as I walked to my room.

Boston was definitely like another world. Overwhelming, but exciting at the same time. Thankfully, Pa used the Boston accent, which helped me understand these people's odd speech! I unpacked my clothes and hung the dresses on the hooks. I put the rest of my belongings in the chest of drawers, except my journal and pencil, which I put on the nightstand next to the kerosene lamp. I would write in it tonight. I hoped I would find my grandfather soon. Maybe tomorrow?

The Family Business

I thoroughly enjoyed bathing in the tub. It was like washing up in the river, but much cleaner. Letting all that water go out seemed like quite a waste though. Same with the sink. *And, where did all that water come from? The ocean?* I wondered. I put on the light blue dress Mrs. Witherspoon gave me, tied up my hair with a scarf, pulled on my boots, collected my rent and board money, and rushed downstairs to meet Mallory.

I heard voices in the kitchen. "Well, what did you expect, Mallory?"

A young voice said, "I don't know. I thought it would be a good idea, I guess."

I stood, silent, in the kitchen doorway. I hated to interrupt, but Mrs. McCarthy turned around and saw me. "Oh, Emeline! Hello. My, don't you look nice in that blue dress." She looked at her daughter. "Mallory, meet Emeline. She'll be our guest for the next month."

"Hello, Emeline," said Mallory.

"Hello, Mallory. I'm happy to meet you." I turned to Mrs. McCarthy and said, "Here's my month's rent and first week's board."

"Thank you, Emeline." She pocketed the money and looked at Mallory. "Why don't you give her a tour of the house, dear?"

"Come, Emeline, let me show you around. Of course, you know this is the kitchen. What are we having for supper, Mama?"

"Beef stew and rolls, tea to drink, and cake for dessert."

"Yum!" said Mallory.

I smiled and followed her to the next room, where she said, "Now this is the dining room. This long table can hold up to ten people at once. It doubles as a library. You can read any of the books you want, but they must stay in this room."

"There are lots of books, I see. Do you have a favorite?"

"I'd have to say, Mark Twain's book, *Adventures of Huckleberry Finn*. I like Robert Lewis Stevenson's book *Treasure Island* too. What about you?"

"I like both of those books, and *Little Women*. I love to read."

"This next room is the parlor; you came through this one earlier. Some people like to come in here after supper to visit. Mama and I both play the piano, but not unless we're asked. It's rude to play unless the others in the room want to hear it. If no one is in the room, then we can play if we want to."

"No one is here right now. Would you play one song for me?"

Smiling, she took her seat on the piano bench and played a little song for me. "That was called *He Was Such a Nice Man*."

"Thank you. You play very well. I've never tried. There aren't many pianos in Kearney, Missouri."

"I've been playing since I was six. I enjoy the piano. Well, there are steps that lead down into the cellar, but we don't need to go there.

That's mostly for storage. Let's go upstairs." We climbed up the stairs to the second floor where my room was. "You know this floor already. There's your room - just to the right of the bathroom. I know you've seen that. The other guests you'll meet at supper: Mr. and Mrs. Spengler live in the room up the hall from yours, Mr. Baldwin's room is across the hall from theirs, and Miss Erica Eckhart lives in the room on the left side of the bathroom."

"And what's upstairs? Your rooms?"

"Yaw, I'll show you where we sleep." We climbed the stairs up to the third floor, which looked almost like the second. "We sleep up here. This is my room." It was the first door on the right and twice the size of the rooms on the second floor. "It's much larger than yours. We made those rooms smaller on purpose so we could take more boarders. Across the hall is Mama and Papa's room. And then there's another bathroom at the end of this floor for us."

"This is very nice! Thank you for showing me the house. Where did Mr. McCarthy go with Penny and the carriage?"

"Oh, at the end of the block there's a livery stable for everyone's horses and carriages or buggies. Mr. Zuckerman and his son James, we call him Jimmy, take care of Penny for us."

"Oh, I see. Do you ever ride Penny? I'd love to do that sometime."

"We'd have to go out of town quite a ways to find some clear roads to travel, but we can ask Papa. Maybe on a fair Saturday we can."

The sound of a bell rang throughout the house.

"That'll be supper. Let's go," said Mallory. "We'll have to look at the fourth floor another time."

Everyone in the house gathered at the long table with a white Battenburg lace covering. In front of me was my place setting: a large bowl, a small plate on top of a slightly larger one at the upper left, a glass tumbler at the upper right, a soup spoon and butter knife to the right of the bowl, and a dessert fork to the left of the bowl. Under the dessert fork was a cloth napkin. The stew was in a ceramic pot on the sideboard along with a chocolate cake on a stand. Mr. McCarthy prayed: "Dear Father in heaven, thank you for this day and this good food. May it nourish our bodies so we are able to continue doing the work you would have us do. Thank you for your Word and your Son. In Jesus' name, Amen."

Mrs. McCarthy stood up and said, "Everyone on my left, please take your bowls and fill them with stew. Then everyone on my right follow them." After all were seated, Mr. and Mrs. McCarthy filled their bowls and sat. We passed the basket of hot rolls around, then the pitchers of tea and water, the salt and pepper shakers, and finally, the butter dish.

After one or two bites, I said, "This is an excellent stew, Mrs. McCarthy." Everyone else agreed and made mumbling noises as it was considered impolite to talk while eating. When the food was gone, Mallory cut the cake and we all got up again to get a piece on the larger plate. All the other dishes were pushed toward the center of the table. When the cake was gone, we each gathered our own dishes: large plate, small plate, bowl, glass, and silverware, and took them to the kitchen where we cleaned them in warm water using soap and a cloth, and then stacked them on a wooden table for Mrs. McCarthy to put away.

Fatigued from the long train ride, I elected to go to bed rather than stay up and visit in the parlor. "I need some sleep, so I'll say good night," I said to Mr. and Mrs. McCarthy and Mallory.

"After breakfast Monday, I'll take you to the library to look for O'Conner Lithography," Mr. McCarthy said. "You're welcome to join us for church in the morning."

"That will be grand," I said. "Thank you."

Once ready for bed, I sat in it with my journal open and pencil ready. I wrote to myself this time:

Saturday evening, May 10, 1890

Dear me, what are you doing, and why?

- I do want to get to know my grandfather, personally, for myself as well as fulfilling my promise to Pa.

- I'm reading the Bible (which is now lost) and learning more about Jesus the more I read.

- But what have I learned on this journey?

- I've learned to make important decisions on my own and I've been thinking about what I really want beyond obedience to and honor of a promise.

- I've learned that Jesus is real and is with me always. He is my best friend and ultimate advisor. Whenever I pray now, it's not something I do for someone else. It's for me.

Thank you for your provision, Father, I love you. Amen.

I closed the journal and laid it on the nightstand with the pencil. The pillow and cotton quilt were soft and comforting. I slept.

Sunday morning was special. Most in the boarding house went to church. Breakfast was simple: toast with butter and jam, and strawberries. There was no ceremony, just come and eat at will.

I woke up early and dressed in my favorite dress; the one with the rosebuds that Ma made with me. I brushed my hair and pulled it up and back with the sage scarf. I brushed my teeth and descended downstairs. Mallory was already in the kitchen getting her breakfast. "Good morning," I said.

"Good morning. Help yourself and come to the table." She glided into the dining room with her plate of toast and strawberries.

"That's a very pretty dress," I said to her. "It's more intricate than any of mine." It was mainly white with navy blue braided trimmings and an anchor embroidered on the sailor style bib. She even wore a white hat with a huge navy blue bow on the front.

"Thank you. The sleeves are called mutton sleeves because they're so puffed on the top, but tight on the forearm; like a leg of lamb, I guess. But, I love your dress."

"Thank you. My ma and I made it together."

"Would you like some apple juice?" She poured it from a pitcher on the table into a small glass. Several glasses circled the pitcher.

"Yes, please. This is delicious. Where are your parents?"

"Mama is upstairs. She's already eaten. Papa is getting Penny and the carriage. He'll be here in just a few minutes. Did you sleep well?"

"I'll say I did. I don't even remember dreaming." We chatted for a bit and then cleaned our dishes, dried them, and stacked them neatly in the kitchen.

Mr. McCarthy marched through the front door and into the parlor. "Good morning, ladies," he said to both of us. He looked at me. "Ready to go to church?"

"Yes, sir. Ready."

Mrs. McCarthy descended the staircase; a beautiful vision in a white flowing skirt with a green leaf print, dark green blouse, and white hat with green ribbons. "Good morning."

Mr. McCarthy took her hand and kissed it. "You look lovely, dear."

Together in the carriage, we rolled down the cobblestone streets and pulled up in front of a gigantic stone church building with many colorful, ornate stained-glass windows.

"It must hold hundreds of people!" In Kearney, we either met at a small country church or someone's home on Sunday.

The McCarthys chuckled.

"Yaw, it does," Mr. McCarthy said.

After church, most of the residents met in the parlor, or helped Mrs. McCarthy with supper. Mallory and I decided to help in the kitchen. The night before, she had made bread dough and put it in the food pantry to rise. Now she just kneaded it one more time, divided it into three parts, rolled it out into three long ropes, and then braided them together, tucking the ends underneath. "Mallory, will you put more coal in the stove please?" she asked.

"Coal?"

"Yaw. Don't you use coal in Kearney?" Mallory asked as she used a scoop to lift black nuggets from an unusual shaped bucket. Mostly round, one side was flattened so you could pour the coal straight from it. She opened the top of the coal box, which was already hot, and added the new coal. "It's called anthracite coal. It doesn't smoke a lot and burns with a blue flame."

"I see. So, is it better than burning wood?"

"Well, here in Boston, we don't have an abundance of wood like you do farther west, but there are many coal mines near here: Pennsylvania, West Virginia, and probably more places than that. Plus the coal only needs to be added every twelve hours or so, once you have a good hot bed of it."

"I need to add new wood about every three or four hours to our stove."

"Right. So a wood stove is more work really."

Soon, supper was prepared and ready and Mrs. McCarthy asked me to ring the bell. Ding-ding, ding-ding. It was a melodic sound. Everyone gathered, prayed, and enjoyed the Sunday meal.

Afterward, Mallory and I spent the rest of the afternoon up on the fourth floor – "The attic room" she called it. It was a warmer room, so we opened up the windows to let in some fresh air. We laughed, shared our stories, and played games until dinner, which was small. Supper was the big meal on Sunday. Then it was off to bed again. Mr. McCarthy let me borrow his Bible for the night so I turned to read what Jesus said about prayer.

Matthew 7:7-12

7 *"Ask and it shall be given you; seek, and ye shall find; knock, and it shall be opened unto you:*

8 *For every one that asketh receiveth; and he that seeketh findeth; and to him that knocketh it shall be opened.*

9 *Or what man is there of you, whom if his son ask bread, will he give him a stone?*

10 *Or if he ask a fish, will he give him a serpent?*

11 *If ye than, being evil, know how to give good gifts unto your children, how much more shall your Father which is in heaven give good things to them that ask him?*

12 *Therefore all things whatsoever ye would that men should do to you, do ye even so to them: for this is the law and the prophets."*

I wrote:

Dear Jesus, thank you for your provision and protection. Please help me find Grandfather Silas tomorrow and please, if it be your will, let him accept me as his own granddaughter. I thank you. Amen.

I slept soundly through the night. In the morning, I heard the rustling of the other renters getting ready and going off to work. When they had finished, I did my ablution and dressed. This time I chose the olive green calico dress with the yellow sash and hair-tie scarf. I put a few coins in my pocket, just in case. "Later today, I must ask Mrs. McCarthy about where I can do my wash," I said to myself. Looking up toward heaven, I said to God, "Please lead me to my grandfather today. Amen."

I hurried downstairs and ate a quick breakfast. Mr. McCarthy was smoking his pipe and waiting for me in the parlor.

"Ready?" he asked.

"Yes, sir, ready."

Penny pulled us all the way to the center of Boston, to the library.

I looked at its edifice: a large stone building with high Gothic arched windows. "It's amazing!"

"Wait till you see the inside."

We pulled Penny to the side, tied her to a hitching post, and traversed the road and sidewalk until we were inside. The main reading room was filled with several long tables, surrounded by wooden chairs, and lit by hanging lanterns. Between the windows were tall bookcases with thousands of books and a rolling ladder on each side to get to the taller shelves. At one end was a fireplace and at the other end was a large desk behind which were rows and rows of little drawers. We approached the desk. Mr. McCarthy motioned for me to make my request as he perused the books.

"Pardon, I am in search of my grandfather. May I inquire as to the whereabouts of a company called O'Connor Lithography?" I asked. There were postcards with pictures of the library on the desk for sale. "And, I'd like to purchase twelve of these cards, please."

The librarian rose from her chair and walked over to a row of books titled *The U.S. Census.* Next to that was the *Boston City Directory: 1890.* This was the book she brought to the desk. "Everyone who lives here is listed by name. I can also provide an address. Let's see, O'Connor, O'Connor." She flipped through the pages, her index finger searching the listings. "What is the first name?"

"Silas," I said.

"I have a listing for Silas O'Connor living at a residence at 35 Washington St., South Boston, Massachusetts. His entry says he is a lithographer."

My heart fluttered. "Would you please write that down for me?"

"Certainly. Let me check the business directory in the back." She turned to that section. "O'Connor Lithography. Here it is. It's the same address. He probably lives in an apartment above the business."

"Thank you so much! You don't know what this means to me."

"Happy to be of assistance to you. The postcards come to twenty-four cents please."

"Would you happen to have any Bibles to sell? I lost mine on my journey."

"No, I'm sorry. But you can find one at the Corner Bookstore on Washington Street."

"Thank you. You've been most helpful." I gathered the postcards and slipped them in my pocket, along with the address. I nodded to Mr. McCarthy and we returned to Penny and the carriage.

"Could we please stop at the Corner Bookstore on Washington Street? The librarian said I could find a Bible there."

"Yaw, I know exactly where it is. Where is your grandfather's business?"

I showed him the address.

"Why, that's just a few blocks from our house. You can walk that distance easily."

"Really? That's incredible! I'll go right after supper."

We stopped at the bookstore and were home by noon. I ran upstairs to wash my face and hands and brushed my hair again. My new Bible now lay on my nightstand, along with the postcards and my journal. I looked up at the ceiling. "Thank you, Lord, again, for your provision. Amen."

After lunch, I brushed my teeth and filled up my canteen with water while Mr. McCarthy drew a map of the streets in the area up to grandfather's address. Anticipation welled up inside. "Thank you, Mr. McCarthy. Thank you for everything."

I scampered out the door and down the street, following the directions on my map. Within fifteen minutes, I stood in front of his building. "Help me, Lord." I climbed the stairs, pushed the door handle down, and leaned against the heavy door. It creaked as it opened and while I turned to shut it, a man wearing an apron over a suit came over to greet me.

"May I help you?" he asked. He was holding sheets of paper under one arm.

"Um. My name is Emeline O'Connor, daughter of Tavis O'Connor of Missouri. I'm seeking my grandfather, please." My hands perspired while my mouth was dry.

"Tavis is my older brother. The name is Trevor O'Connor." He shook my hand and smiled. "That makes you my niece!"

Pa had a brother? How did I not know this? "How do you do." I smiled, grateful for his immediate acceptance.

"But where is my brother? Isn't he with you?"

"No. It's a long story, but I'm sorry to tell you, your brother, my pa, has died. He asked me to come and find my grandfather. It was important to him that I connect with our family."

"Oh, no! How did that happen?"

"I think it was his heart. Farming is hard physical work."

"I'm sorry to hear that. But it's odd that he felt that way, about family, after he, himself, left us so many years ago."

"I wondered that too. I guess he thought I needed family to take care of me, as I'm only thirteen."

"Your grandfather, Silas, is up in years. He's feeble and struggles with his hearing, vision, and memory. Unable to work in the shop, he lives in an apartment on the third floor of this building. I run the business now, and my wife and I have our hands full with four small children. If you plan to stay, we'll have to discuss living arrangements and so forth."

"I understand."

"You might be just what we need at our house; a helper with the little ones at home. It's good to meet you. I can see Tavis in your eyes," he said, as his eyes met mine.

Pleased with that compliment, I smiled. "Would you mind if I visited Grandfather Silas?"

"I don't mind, but his mood and memory are usually best in the *morning*. Better try tomorrow."

"Alright. I'll return then."

He opened the door for me and I shuffled down the steps.

"See you tomorrow morning," he said.

I waved and started back to the boarding house. A helper with the young children? My eyes stung with tears that wanted to fall. I let them.

Silas

It was a good thing I had a long walk before I arrived at the McCarthys. So much emotion needed to vent. For now, I decided to focus on my immediate needs: clean clothes and time to clear my head. I looked at my pocket watch: three o'clock. "Mrs. McCarthy, where may I wash my clothes?"

"There's a bench wringer out back in the courtyard. I'll show you. You'll need hot water. Fill up this tall pan about halfway with water and set it on the stove."

I did this and then we walked out the kitchen door. "Oh, this is lovely!" This was the first I'd seen of the courtyard between the residences. Stone walkways outlined the courtyard center, which was grassy and green with small gardens and large trees. Children were playing on two, no three, swing sets and a seesaw. "What are those women doing?"

"Playing croquet. A ball is struck with a mallet with a long handle and it must go through the wire wickets. The goal is to go from one side to the other, hit the post, and return again to the original post."

"I see. And what game are those people playing?"

"Tennis. Two or four players volley a light, soft-covered ball with a racquet back and forth until it drops to the ground more than once or goes out of bounds. A server starts the volley and keeps the serve until they fail to return it or win the game. If they fail to return it, the serve goes to the other player or team. The game has only four points, but the winner must win by two, so sometimes the games can last a long time."

"What fun! Mallory and I should come out here after dinner."

"She would love that. There could be some other young friends outside that she could introduce you to as well. Here's the wash area. This bench holds a wringer between two washtubs. This washtub holds the washboard for washing with soap. The soap is in the kitchen under the sink. Then you send your clean clothes through the wringer and it will go into the rinse tub. After a second time through the wringer, you can hang them on the clothesline to dry. The clothespins are in a bag, which is hanging on the line. Is this how you've washed clothes before?"

"Basically, yes. Thank you, Mrs. McCarthy. I'll go change into one of my riding outfits and wash my underpinnings and dresses. It's a nice, warm day. If I wash now, they should be dry before bedtime."

"I'll leave you to it."

After hanging my wash, I had a little time before dinner. There was one more place I wanted to visit: the livery stable. I strolled down the sidewalk to the end of the block. The doors were open to the livery stable. Outside, a man in a leather apron hammered on horseshoes next to a blazing fire pit.

I approached him and said, "Hello."

His face, blackened by the smoke, turned toward me. The contrast between his light blue eyes and smoky face was startling. "Hey there, young lady. May I help you?"

"I am staying at the McCarthys and just wanted to see where Penny lives."

"Penny? Sure, come on in." He trudged over the dirt floor. "My name's Mr. Zuckerman. And yours is?"

"Emeline O'Connor." I followed him into the huge barn. There must have been twenty large horse stalls. The smell of fresh straw, hay, and horses was heavy, but delightful to me. A young man was distributing feed: oats and barley. Buckets of fresh water hung in each stall, along with that horse's tack.

"James, come and meet Miss Emeline O'Connor." Mr. Zuckerman led us down to the end of the long barn. In the last stall, the biggest of all stalls, was Penny. Mr. Zuckerman left us to return to his blacksmithing.

"Oh, isn't she beautiful?" I said.

James said, "Are you used to being around horses? Would you like to fill her grain bin?"

"Yes, I am. Could I?"

James' dark brown hair was short and swept up in front for a clear view of his amber eyes and dark brows. He had the beginning of a mustache too and looked a little older than I, maybe about the same age as Jonathan. He handed me the bucket, opened the stall door, and approached Penny, letting her know he was there by touching her rump and gliding it over her side. I stayed to the side until I reached her bin. "How much?"

"Two scoops will do," he said. "I just filled her hay rack and water too, so she'll be happy with that. Would you like to brush her?"

"Will she allow it?"

"Yaw, she's a sweet mare. Very patient and gentle. Here." He handed me the currycomb.

Gently, at first, I brushed her neck and shoulders. "I'd need a step to reach her back. She's so tall!"

"Here." He handed me a stepstool, stepped back and leaned against the stall wall to watch me. "She's a Clydesdale."

More aggressively, I brushed her back from her withers down her spine and over her rump. Then I brushed her dark mane, tail, and finally, the long white hair near her feet. I sighed deeply. There was something relaxing for me about being with a horse.

"You're different from most Boston girls. Where are you from?"

"Kearney, Missouri: nine states away! I have a Morgan horse named Dakota that I had to leave in Indianapolis on my way. I sure do miss him."

"Understandable. I get attached to certain horses we take care of. Penny's one of them," he said.

"Well, you certainly take good care of them. Does she get exercised? I'd love to ride her sometime."

"You'd have to talk to the owner, Mr. McCarthy. That would be up to him. But yaw, he usually takes Penny out for a ride or to a nearby pasture to let her run at least once or twice a week, in addition to her carriage duties."

"Where are the carriages?"

"They're in a carriage house around the corner."

"Yaw, she's a sweet mare. Very patient and gentle. Here."
He handed me the currycomb.

"I see. Well, thank you for letting me visit. I should be getting back now."

"It was my pleasure. Enjoy your stay and come by anytime."

Back at the McCarthys I checked my laundry on the line. It was still damp but the breeze would dry it quickly. I would need to eat dinner in my riding outfit. In my room, I brushed my hair and washed my hands. The dinner bell would ring soon.

Ding, ding. Ding, ding. *There it is. I'm hungry too.* I scurried downstairs and took my place at the long table. Tonight we ate seafood: cod filets. And something they called chips, which were thin sliced potatoes fried in oil. I can tell you this would be a delicacy in Kearney, but in Boston, it was very common. Delicious.

Afterward, in the parlor, I asked, "Mallory, could we visit the seaside sometime?"

She turned to her parents. "Could we?" she asked them.

"Absolutely, we'll all go this weekend if the weather's nice," said Mr. McCarthy. "I don't have any work at the YMCA this Saturday. How did your visit go today, Emeline?"

I explained I would have to return in the morning and the reasons why. "I'm not hopeful this trip will end the way Pa wanted it to."

"I'm sorry about that. Maybe it's for the best," he said. Thankfully, he didn't ask any more questions.

"Mallory, let's go out to the courtyard. I'd love to swing for awhile, and I need to bring in my laundry too."

"Alright."

We swung up high, chattering, laughing, and having a grand time. It was good to be outside where it was green and open, even if it was in a limited space. "Want to see our garden?" Mallory asked.

"Yes."

We strode over to the little garden near where my laundry hung. In it grew string beans, peas, lettuce, and carrots. Bordering the garden were marigolds, which had a strong odor, but were bright orange and yellow. "It's probably nothing like where you're from, but I love to come out and pick the vegetables and clear the rows of weeds. The flowers are pretty, and their smell keeps animals from eating our plants and produce."

"It's very nice, and you're correct. Our farm is one hundred and sixty acres of the blackest dirt you ever saw. It takes a lot of work to plant, maintain, and harvest that much." My mind drifted into memories of Ma and Pa.

"It isn't much, but it's enough for us. It's a special treat to have fresh vegetables. We don't enjoy them all year. In the winter, mostly we have potatoes, turnips, onions, carrots, apples, beets, and rutabagas. Sometimes we have cabbage. Mama has a good friend who has a large garden and cans her fruits and vegetables. She goes there and helps her harvest and preserve in exchange for lots of jars of the food. By October, our pantry is chock full."

"I'm glad she has that friend. Thank you for coming out tonight." I unpinned my clothes from the line and draped them over my arm. "I think I'll get ready for bed now and turn in early."

"It was fun. We'll do it again. Good night, Emeline."

In my room, I hung up the dresses and folded the underpinnings. I slipped out of my riding clothes and hung them up too, and pulled on the nightgown Mrs. McCarthy had loaned me. Since night had fallen, I lit the oil lamp on the nightstand.

The quiet of the night enveloped me. I watched the flicker of the flame in the glass chimney and played with the knob on the side of the lamp. The flame grew tall if I turned it up, or very small if I turned it down. I didn't want to waste the oil or wick, so I turned it just high enough so that I could read and write. I opened the Bible to Matthew 6:25-27.

25 *Therefore I say unto you, Take no thought for your life, what ye shall eat, or what ye shall drink; nor yet for your body, what ye shall put on. Is not the life more than meat, and the body than raiment?*

26 *Behold the fowls of the air: for they sow not, neither do they reap, nor gather into barns; yet your heavenly Father feedeth them. Are ye not much better than they?*

27 *Which of you by taking thought can add one cubit unto his stature?*

Monday evening, May 12, 1890

Dear Lord, thank you for this day and for the excellent family you have led me to. Please be with me tomorrow when I meet Grandfather Silas. May I be a blessing to him in some way. Amen.

I set the Bible and my journal down for a moment and pondered these verses. I can't add measure to my life, but my heavenly Father can – and does. He places me in situations and around certain people to add to my growth.

I always thought that other *people* made my life secure. Ma, Pa, Harriet, Miss Ambrose, the Witherspoons, now the McCarthys, and more. And some other *people* made my life insecure, like that horrible man, Jeb and Mr. Phillips. Now, as I thought about it further, I realized that my security doesn't come from *people* at all. It comes from Jesus! So, that means my fear of insecurity has no foundation at all. I wanted to read more of Matthew 6.

28 *And why take ye thought for raiment? Consider the lilies of the field, how they grow; they toil not, neither do they spin:*

29 *And yet I say unto you, That even Solomon in all his glory was not arrayed like one of these.*

30 *Wherefore, if God so clothe the grass of the field, which to day is, and to morrow is cast into the oven, shall he not much more clothe you, O ye of little faith?*

I looked at my clothes: one dress was mine, two were given to me, and the robe and nightgown were loaned. I kept reading.

31 *Therefore take no thought, saying, What shall we eat? Or, What shall we drink? Or, Wherewithal shall we be clothed?*

32 *(For after all these things do the Gentiles seek:) for your heavenly Father knoweth that ye have need of all these things.*

33 *But seek ye first the kingdom of God, and his righteousness; and all these things shall be added unto you.*

34 *Take therefore no thought for the morrow: for the morrow shall take thought for the things of itself. Sufficient until the day is the evil thereof.*

That means I need not worry about the future either! I need only take one day at a time, and know, really believe, that Jesus will take care of me. I placed the Good Book and my journal back on the nightstand and turned off the lantern. In the darkness, I said to Jesus, "I never understood before, but I do now. I will keep reading to get to know you even better. Thank you for your Word and for giving me peace inside. Amen." *Tomorrow will be a good day, no matter what.*

In the morning, I put on my favorite dress, the one with the pink rosebuds. I ate a quick breakfast and headed to O'Connor Lithography. I arrived early: eight o'clock by my watch.

I stood inside the door and waited. The room was large with a high ceiling and full of equipment, supplies, and a few people working.

One man was at a sort of easel desk. Another was drawing on what looked like a stone with some kind of marking tool. Others were setting up what I imagined were printing presses, carefully aligning the paper as they put it on the press. Still others milled about. From the midst I saw my Uncle Trevor. He gazed in my direction; I waved. After giving a few more directions, he came over. "Good morning, Emeline. I hope you had a nice evening."

"Yes, thank you. How's Grandfather Silas this morning? Is he awake?"

"He is awake, but he's being tended to now by Miss Perkins who helps me with him. She's getting him ready for your visit. He's eating breakfast at the moment. While you wait, would you like a tour?"

"I'd love to learn about the family business. Thank you."

"I thought you might. We'll start at the beginning. An artist draws a picture and colors it. It might be for an advertisement, or a label, or perhaps a large poster. The most important thing is to note the number of colors in the artwork. The fewer the colors, the easier it is to print. You see, each color is printed separately. And some colors are printed on top of each other to make a new color, like green, for example. It's blue printed over yellow."

"Oh, that's fascinating. So, some colors are printed side by side, some overlap, and some areas have no color and stay white."

"Exactly. And, sometimes, we stipple the colors, which means we just print tiny dots of one color near tiny dots of another. Close up, you can see them separately, but from a distance, they look like a third color such as red and yellow dots looking somewhat orange or flesh-tone."

"I never noticed that before."

"That's the idea. Unless you look closely, your eye mixes the two colors. Stippling is a tedious job and is usually given to an apprentice."

"Another consideration is the order of the colors to be printed. You can't print them all willy-nilly. There must be a plan."

I listened attentively. It was quite an art.

"Now, this gentleman is a lithographic designer who takes the work of art, analyzes the number of colors, and the order for printing, and creates plates: one for each color. The plates are really stones, and this grease pencil is the tool he uses to draw with. The ink will adhere to the grease, and later we will wet the stone, which will prevent the ink from going anywhere else. But I'm getting ahead of myself."

"It sounds complicated."

"It *is* technical. I'll try to keep it simple. This worker is the proofer. He double-checks the work of the designer by doing a test on one sheet of paper with all the stones. The key is to get the registration pinpointed. If one color doesn't line up where it's supposed to, the print is worthless. He makes tiny marks on the stones so later at the press, all the colors will register correctly on the paper."

"I would imagine that if only three or four colors were used, that would be a less expensive print than one of, say, eight colors, right?"

"Yaw, that's right. You understand business. Most of our customers are advertisers and use just the primary colors, but there are a few that will pay the extra amount."

"Let's move on to the the press. We have five of the newest ones. They are capable of handling larger stones, and larger sheets of paper. And, they use rollers instead of scrapers, which is an improvement."

"This is an enormous machine. Look at all the knobs and intricate moving parts!"

"It's the pressman's job to get the paper lined up exactly right. The paper goes at this end and is held by small pins. The first color stone is on the other end. It is wetted down and then inked with the first color. The ink is oil-based so only sticks to the greased parts. As you probably know, oil and water don't mix."

"Yes."

"Then the paper, secured in a frame, is slid over and just above the wet stone. Finally, these rollers roll from one end of the press to the other, and push the stone and paper together. Wherever the ink touches the paper, it sticks. Then it is removed and set aside to dry. We can make many of this one color print before we have to re-ink the stone."

"How long does it take to dry?"

"Well, it depends a lot on the humidity in the air. On a hot day, it doesn't take long. On a rainy day, it does take awhile. The most difficult part is that the paper actually swells with each pass. So, sometimes, we have to wait days for the paper to shrink back down before we can do the next colors. It just depends on the air. As I say, if it's not exactly registered, it's worthless."

"There's a lot more to it than I imagined. Thank you, Uncle Trevor."

"I'll check to see if Grandfather Silas is ready. Stay right here and watch the pressman. I'll be back shortly."

I watched the others work while I waited. They all seemed to take pride in their work.

"He's ready. Come with me," Uncle Trevor said. I was nervous at this first meeting, finally imminent. I climbed the wooden staircase following Uncle Trevor closely. The third floor was separated into several rooms. "This is Miss Perkins. Miss Perkins, this is Emeline O'Connor. I will come back later." He returned to work.

"Nice to meet you. I'm here to visit Grandfather Silas," I said.

"Yaw, please come in," she said. "I'll be nearby if you need me. Remember, his memory isn't good."

Seated in a wheelchair was Grandfather Silas. He stared at me with uncertainty. "Who are you?"

"Hello. I'm Emeline, your son Tavis' girl, your granddaughter."

He cleared his throat and said, "Who?"

"My name is Emeline. Do you remember your son, Tavis?"

"Tavis, Tavis. You mean Trevor? Aye, he's me son. Handles the business now. Are you his daughter?"

"No. Do you remember your *older* son, Tavis, who moved west to Missouri to farm?"

"What was your name? Elizabeth?"

"No, sir. It's Emeline. Emeline."

"Emeline. That's a pretty name. Do you want to set down and visit? I don't get many visitors anymore." He pulled himself up straight in the wheelchair and spread a quilt over his lap.

"Yes, thank you." I sat in a wooden chair with an upholstered seat cushion across from Grandfather Silas. *Maybe I could help him remember if we talked about him*, I thought. With a strong Irish accent, Grandfather's speech was very different, so I had to pay close attention to understand him. "You have quite a good business downstairs. When did you start it?"

"Ahh, me. Well, that was a long time ago now. Let's see. Hmm. I don't recollect the year, but my wife and I started it just after we were married. Me father was a lithographer in Ireland and I started it here to Boston."

"Do you like America better than Ireland?"

"Ahh, I miss the old country sometimes. Business is better here in Boston. There are so many more opportunities. I used to get out all the time and visit other businesses." His eyes wandered to the pictures on the wall.

"Tell me about your family. Did you and your wife have children?"

"Aye, we had two sons. The one that brought you up here, that's Trevor."

"And the other?"

"The other was our first born. He left us when he was just seventeen. Said he didn't want to live in Boston anymore. Too crowded. Wanted to farm someplace out west." He rubbed his chin. "Never understood that boy."

"Missouri?"

"Maybe. I don't remember. I haven't heard from him in years."

"What was his name?"

"Tavis."

"Tavis! That's right. What do you remember about him?"

"Well, let's see. I remember his boyhood games and such; such a strapping, good-looking boy. He met a girl, what was her name? Well, no matter. They fell in love, I guess, got married and moved west."

"Do you remember giving him anything to take with him?"

"She was beautiful, that girl, much like you are." He chuckled. "I think her name was Kate, but I'm not sure."

"Yes, that's right. Tavis and Kate. Did he take anything to remember you by? Something he might have treasured that you shared?"

"Aye, let's see. I gave him me Bible. That was mostly to remember his mother though. We used to hunt rabbits in the country when he was a boy. There was a gun that we had both initialed, and a knife, I think." He stared at the floor. "Ahh, and me father's pocket watch. That was extra special to me. I hope he takes good care of it."

A pocket watch? "Does it look like this?" I unpinned it from my pocket and handed it to him.

"Why aye, aye, this is it!" He turned the watch over and opened the back. Inside there was an inscription.

To Silas with love from William O'Connor ~ 1840

"How did you come by it?" He handed it back to me.

I never knew about that back inscription. I pinned it back in my pocket. "I'm your granddaughter, Emeline, daughter of your son Tavis and his wife Kate." His eyes caught mine and started to fill with joyful tears.

"Come here and let me hold your hands. I never thought I would see you. Tavis wrote about you, though it's been a long time ago now. Ahh, how are they; Tavis and Kate?"

"I'm sorry, Grandfather. Ma, Kate, died during childbirth along with the baby two years ago. And Pa died only two months ago of heart problems. Before he passed he asked me to come to see you. He said I should have courage and that family is important."

"Oh, no." He paused for a moment. "Emeline, is it? Such a lovely name for a lovely granddaughter. I'm sorry to hear about your parents' passing. Poor Tavis. Poor Kate. You must have had quite a long journey. Were you alone?"

"Yes, mostly. If you'd like to hear it, I can tell you the story. I kept a journal and could read that to you too."

"There's nothing I'd like better than to have regular visits from me granddaughter. You can read anything you like to me. Me years have caught up with me and I can't read much anymore."

"I'd love to hear your stories about our family, especially about you and Pa."

Toward the door, Grandfather Silas called out, "Miss Perkins! Come meet me granddaughter, Emeline O'Connor."

"Why aye, aye, this is it!" He turned the watch over and opened the
back. Inside there was an inscription.

Family at Last

That night, I wrote postcards to Harriet, Miss Ambrose, Mr. Pickwick, Ole Mr. Thompson, the Coopers, and now the Witherspoons with my update:

I made it safely to Boston by train and am staying with my new friends, the McCarthy family, in their boarding house. And, I found Grandfather Silas! I'll be staying here to get to know him for awhile. I'll keep you posted. Love, Emeline

As I wrote each of these postcards I thought about the recipients. I missed them terribly, not that I have any regrets. On the contrary, this trip has been exciting on many levels: physically, emotionally, and, yes, spiritually. I'm glad I fulfilled my promise to Pa. And, I'm looking forward to reading to and talking with Grandfather Silas. While Boston is a mecca filled with modern advances as well as historic interest, I miss the sky. I miss the openness of the country. And, I miss my friends. In my journal, I wrote:

Dear Lord, thank you for bringing me this far and leading me to Grandfather Silas. It seems clear to me that what I need to do now is finish out my month with the McCarthys and establish a relationship with Grandfather Silas through daily visits and then return to Indianapolis. I'm so happy that he remembered Pa, finally, through the pocket watch. Please help him remember me tomorrow. And, please show me a way to finance my trip west. Amen.

With a deep breath of satisfaction, I lay the journal on the nightstand and opened my Bible to read Matthew 8. My eyes grew heavy and my mind fuzzy. I lay the Book on the journal, snuggled up in the quilt, and slept.

Wednesday morning, I washed, dressed in my light blue dress, and went down for breakfast around eight o'clock. I enjoyed a small bowl of oatmeal with raisins, milk, and some fresh grapes. Mrs. McCarthy was doing some laundry outside with Mallory, so I joined them for a moment. "Good morning!"

"Good morning, Emeline. How are you today?" Mrs. McCarthy asked.

"Good morning," said Mallory.

"Fine, thank you. I have a question for you."

Taking the clothespin out of her mouth to hang up a towel, she said, "What's that?"

"I was wondering if you need any help with laundry – or even if others that live here might pay me a little to do their laundry? I've decided after my month is up, I will return to Indianapolis, and I'll need to earn money for the trip somehow. What do you think?"

"Yaw, I think that's a good idea, Emeline. I would certainly enjoy a little time off to do other things, and I know the residents would be open to the idea too. You'll have to ask them, though," Mrs. McCarthy said.

"I still want to get to know Grandfather Silas and morning is the best time for his visits. But my afternoons will be free. Can you save any laundry for me to do then?"

"Mama, that would give you and me time to do some sewing or reading," Mallory said, smiling.

"Certainly, there's a pile of sheets that need washing. You can take down the towels, fold them neatly, and then wash and hang up the sheets for me. Thank you, Emeline."

"Do you think I'll earn enough to pay for a train ticket to Indianapolis by mid-June?"

"I should think so, but you know, you might ask your grandfather too. He may be able to help. But it's commendable that you're trying to do it yourself." She snapped the towel in the air and pinned the corners to the line.

"One more question: May I borrow, just for each day I visit Grandfather, one of the books from your library to read to him? I promise to bring it back every day. I know this is contrary to your rule of the books staying in the room, though. I don't want to disrespect you."

"Thank you for your polite request, and since it's for a good cause, I will allow it. Only one book at a time, though. I know you'll take good care of it. Which book did you have in mind?"

"I noticed you have *The Adventures of Huckleberry Finn*. That's the book I was reading to Pa the night before…" My voice trailed off.

"I understand. Of course you may."

"Oh, thank you, Mrs. McCarthy. Well, I'd better be going. I'll see you later for supper. Bye, Mallory."

"Good bye," said Mallory.

"Have a good time," said Mrs. McCarthy.

On my way out, I pulled that title from the bookshelf in the parlor and tucked it under my arm. Stepping down to the sidewalk, I skipped over to the O'Connor Lithography building and arrived in just a few minutes.

Inside the front door, I waited for Uncle Trevor. As usual, he managed the work on the floor, spouting off directions to one person and another. After a few minutes, he reached me. "How are you today, Uncle Trevor?"

"Fine, fine. And you?"

"I'm fine."

"You were the talk of the day yesterday. Your grandfather was happy to meet you, as he will be again today, I'm sure. In fact, he's ready now. Do you remember how to get up to the third floor?"

"Yes, I do."

"Excellent. I'll get back to work. Have a good morning."

I climbed the two staircases up to the top floor and crossed over the main room to his bedroom.

"Good morning, Grandfather."

Silas set down the newspaper and looked at me. "Good morning. Who are you again? You look familiar."

Oh, dear. "I'm your granddaughter, Emeline. We met yesterday, remember?"

"I don't remember much from one day to the next. About all I remember are memories from way back, which is fine for me, but frustrates other people like Miss Perkins and me son, Trevor. I can see it in their faces; like yours now."

I smiled, "I'm sorry. We can start over. May I sit near you?"

"Sure."

"Yesterday morning I was here and you didn't know me, which I knew you wouldn't, but I thought you'd remember my pa, Tavis, your son. Do you remember him now?"

"Tavis, aye, me oldest son. He married a young woman and moved west."

"Right, you remember! I showed you this pocket watch." I took it from my pocket and let him hold it.

"Me father gave me this." He opened the back to look at the inscription again.

I reminded him, "Your father gave that to you. You gave it to your son, Tavis, and he gave it to me, his only child."

"Dat makes you me granddaughter!"

"Yes, Emeline. My name is Emeline."

"Emeline. Such a pretty name. Please remind me, why are you here?"

Patience. I must have some. "Your son, my pa, Tavis, died recently and on his deathbed, he made me promise that I would come see you because being with family is important."

"Tavis passed away?"

"Yes, I'm sorry. Would you like to talk about Tavis? I would love to hear your stories about him."

"He was a good son, always a little different from the rest of us though. He had big dreams that his mother and I didn't understand. But we were set in our ways, and he was young and inspired by the hope of something bigger and better than life here in Boston. I always knew he didn't like working in the shop like Trevor did. Too many details for him. Too much precision. Too many rules."

"I understand. What else?"

"He was in his element whenever we left the city to go hunting, horseback riding, or camping overnight. He loved it there. His eyes widened. He smiled more. We didn't do it too often, but the idea of leaving town for the country excited him. He loved the ocean too. It's just down the street, you know."

"Really? I would love to see the ocean. I haven't seen it yet. May I take you there?"

"I think we could manage. We do have a fierce steam elevator in the building, so I wouldn't have to use the stairs."

"An elevator?" Something else new.

"Miss Perkins!" he shouted toward his doorway.

She appeared, "Yes, sir."

"Ahh, thank you. Miss Perkins, me granddaughter and I want to go see the ocean. Will you help us outside?"

"Certainly, and I'll accompany you but stay a safe distance away so you can visit privately."

"Aye. Let's go. Getting outside might be grand."

Soon, we were on the sidewalk. All we needed to do was roll Grandfather's wheelchair about three blocks to the end of a street, and there it was! An endless view of water and sky, except for a small island and a few sailboats. Way in the distance, past a rocky island, I saw a large steamship with three stacks for the escaping steam. "Is that an island, Grandfather?"

"Aye. That's Fort Independence. It was built there when I was a boy. The fort is in the shape of a pentagon; it has five equal sides with a pretty interesting history. It's still manned today."

Flocks of white birds flew overhead, screeching, and sometimes diving into the water. "What kind of birds are those?"

"Seagulls. They love to catch and eat fish and other seafood that washes ashore."

"Grandfather, do you mind if I go up to the water?"

"Aye, crack on. I'll stay here." He smiled as he watched me run to the ocean.

The water crashed in waves against the shore. Parts of the shore were rocky, and parts were sandy. I took the sandy route and picked up a few seashells on the way. I put them in my pocket for a memory, set my shoes aside, and walked into the shallow waves. The cool salt water and wet sand felt delightful on my bare feet. I stood, arms outstretched, eyes closed, felt the ocean breeze, and smelled the salty air. I listened to the waves wash rhythmically over my feet and legs, and to the seagulls in the air. I loved the open space of water and air and breathed in as much of it as I could.

Turning around, I waved, and Grandfather waved back. Miss Perkins was picking wildflowers nearby. I ran to collect my shoes, and stood by his side as I brushed the sand from my feet and put my shoes back on. "Thank you, Grandfather. I love the ocean. Don't you?"

"Aye. I used to enjoy contemplating on the shore during late afternoons. It's a nice place for that. Or reading. Tavis and I used to go over there about a mile or so to fish. He was a good fisherman. We could eat fish every night in those days. Usually, it was striped bass." We strolled back to the shop, chatting along the way.

Every morning afterward I met with Grandfather and enjoyed his stories as much as he enjoyed mine. We even found time to read all of *The Adventures of Huckleberry Finn*, which he and I relished. The end of the month was in sight, and Grandfather understood my desire to return to Indianapolis after all I shared about it. He surprised me by offering to pay for my railroad ticket! I earned enough anyway from doing laundry in the afternoons, so this was quite a bonus. I couldn't wait to see Dakota, the Witherspoons, and Jonathan again. Grandfather Silas, Penny, and the ocean were glorious distractions in Boston, but, ah, I missed them.

It was nearly mid-June and planning the trip home was done. Grandfather Silas paid for my train ticket: first class! I would enjoy the Pullman cars where the seats were cushioned and everyone had a bunk they could sleep in. And, he included meals.

My clothes were clean and I was packed. Tomorrow, I would be traveling once again. Today, I made my rounds, first to Grandfather, whom I thanked, kissed, and promised I would write. Then, on to the Zuckermans to say good-bye to Penny, Mr. Zuckerman, and James. Finally, after dinner, I said good-bye and gave thanks to the residents and especially to the McCarthy family for helping me.

Clothed in my borrowed nightgown, I leaned against the headboard of my bed, pulled my knees up, and read from Matthew 7:24-25:

"Therefore whosoever heareth these sayings of
mine, and doeth them, I will liken him unto a wise
man, which built his house upon a rock:

And the rain descended, and the floods came, and
the winds blew, and beat upon that house; and it
fell not: for it was founded upon a rock."

Wednesday evening, June 11, 1890

Thank you, Father in heaven, for being my rock. I treasure your words more than anything for I know all blessings come from you. Bless Grandfather Silas, Uncle Trevor, Mr. and Mrs. McCarthy, and Mallory, and all the kind and generous friends I've made during this journey. Please protect me on this return trip and may I be a blessing to the Witherspoon family as we live and work together. In the name of Jesus, amen.

After the night's sleep, restless from anticipation, I hurried to get ready for the day and made sure everything was packed. I hung the nightgown and robe on the back of the bedroom door, and descended downstairs holding my rucksack under my arm. I dropped it in the parlor, spooned some raisin-oatmeal into a bowl, and sat at the table to eat with Mallory and Mrs. McCarthy.

"Have a glass of milk, Emeline." Mrs. McCarthy poured milk into a glass from a pitcher on the table.

"Thank you. I will miss you all, and the modern conveniences of Boston, but I promise to write."

"And we'll write back," said Mallory.

"Good," I said as I gulped the milk down. Where's Mr. McCarthy?"

"Getting Penny and the carriage ready for your trip to the depot." Mallory smiled.

And then it was time. With my rucksack on my back, I stood on the steps outside and looked up and down the street at the tall brick buildings, the cobblestone road, memorizing the features, smells, and sounds. Penny clip-clopped around the corner and Mr. McCarthy pulled her up next to me and said, "Whoa! Good morning, Emeline. Ready?" He hopped down to help me into the front seat.

"Yes, sir!" We were on our way.

Mr. McCarthy dropped me off at the depot. I knew exactly where to go and what to do by now. I gave him a big hug. "I'm so glad I met you on the train earlier. I truly appreciate everything you and your family have done for me this last month. I'll write soon."

"It was our pleasure. Good-bye, Emeline. Be safe," he said with a wave of his hand.

My train was waiting for its passengers to board: departure in twenty minutes. I approached the train, showed the conductor my ticket, and he motioned for me to go to the front of the train— to the first car, as I was traveling first class. I gave that conductor my ticket, which he punched and returned. Offering me his arm for balance, I boarded the car.

You can't imagine the difference between first and third class. This car was like a living room, or parlor, on rails. Ornate ceilings with artwork and lamps accented the length of the car. The curved part of the car near the ceiling had more art, half-circles with paintings, fancy wood trim like the Witherspoons made, and then, underneath that, long doors with embossed artwork on their faces. These were the "bunks" you pull down and sleep on if you want to. Finally, there were the train windows, which were adorned with fancy curtains, and the plush seats that looked like they could seat two. Each seat had diamond, button-tuck upholstery at the top for your head and extravagant decorations embroidered into the lower back. The seat cushion was thick.

Other passengers were dressed like the car: stylish and fancy. I found my way to an empty seat and found I could put my rucksack underneath the seat easily. The conductor came by to make sure all the luggage was put under the seats securely. And then, he made an announcement:

"Ladies and gentlemen. Thank you for selecting the Pullman car for your trip today. We will be traveling west, making several stops until we reach San Francisco, California. If you're going the whole distance, we will be there in about a week. Let me show you how to lower the bunks for sleeping. You simply stand up from your seat and pull down on the handle like this." He demonstrated. "Against the wall, you'll see a netting that you will remove and attach to the outside of your mattress to prevent you from falling off. We have ladders to assist with your ascent."

He continued. "If you are traveling alone, you won't need this. You can simply turn the bottom of your chair over, back to front, on the hidden hinge. Legs will swing out and lock in place to support it. Do the same with the chair opposite you, and you'll have a lovely bed. That's why we only book one person or one couple for every two chairs."

"Finally, we will serve three meals each day in the dining car behind us. You'll cross between the cars through this door. Meals are served for one hour at eight o'clock in the morning, one o'clock, and six o'clock in the evening. Don't be late! There are two small bathrooms: one at the front of this car, and one at the end of the dining car. Knock first before entering, please. I'll be on board if you have any needs. Enjoy your trip!"

"Well, I never...," I said to myself. This was going to be so different from my first trip, which I thought was wonderful. I enjoyed this extravagance and knew I would remember it always.

One and one-half days later, I reached the depot in Indianapolis.

I stepped off the car, thanked the conductor, and looked around for the Witherspoons.

"Emeline!" Mr. Witherspoon raised his hand and ran toward me. Then he gave me a big bear hug. "Welcome home."

My eyes began to water from emotion. "It's great to be here."

At the house, Mrs. Witherspoon rushed out to give me a hug and help me in the house with my things. "We've missed you dreadfully, Emeline."

Not to be left out, Jonathan sprinted from the wood shop, his long legs covering the distance in seconds. Smiling broadly, he too gave me a long hug and a kiss on the forehead. "I've missed you, kid."

Oh, my! My cheeks flushed. "I've missed you too, Jonathan. I can't wait to work together in the shop again." Secretly, I wanted more, but I kept that to myself.

Last, but not least, I scampered over to the fence rail and whistled for Dakota. He galloped over to meet me and whinnied with delight. My hands held his head and my face touched his velvet nose. "It's going to be alright now, Dakota. I'm home, boy."

Elated, I shared the story of my amazing journey with Jonathan and the Witherspoons that first night. As soon as I bought some stationary, I wrote letters, long ones, to everyone in Kearney, especially to Mr. Pickwick about the farm. I asked him to make a deal with the Coopers so they could pay it off a little at a time over many years to finally own the property. Someday I might visit, but my new home was in Indianapolis.

My blissful life continued at the Witherspoons. I learned more about the art of decorative wood carving and became quite proficient at it. Dakota and I rode together whenever we could, even if only to run errands. Seasons moved like a song through the year: *spring* planting, and picnics; *summer* fresh fruits, vegetables, and swimming; *fall* harvest, preservation, and hayrides; *winter* reading, writing, sewing, baking, and bonfires. And, like a chorus, we found time for each other in the evenings and on weekends. Jonathan and I became close friends, even though he was a little older. He helped me with all the activities of the year, when he was available, and could always make me laugh.

One day, as I hung the wash on the clothesline, I recalled doing the same thing in Kearney with Ma and at the McCarthys. Strange how such a simple activity could stimulate memories of other people, places, and times. It made me happy to consider myself part of this new family. A family made, not by blood, but of kindness and generosity.

The End

What Life Was Like in 1890

The Second Industrial Revolution in America spanned the years from 1850 to 1914. This story takes place in the year 1890. Let's take a look at some of the inventions that transformed the everyday lives of Americans then and later.

- HORSE POWER: horses took people where they needed to go, plus they helped pull heavy farm implements, carts, carriages, covered wagons, and omnibuses.

- WIND POWER: used for grinding grain and other farm uses.

- WOOD POWER: used for cooking and heat in the home. Also used for early steam engines until coal replaced it.

- STEAM POWER: steam engines were used for many tools, but also for elevators, trains, ships, and early cars.

- COAL POWER: replaced wood in stoves, lasted longer, and burned cleaner.

- OIL POWER: 1800s lanterns / lamps and making candles.

- GAS POWER: in the late 1800s – early 1900s was used for heat and cooking.

- STEAMBOATS: moved people and products over major river ways bringing the country closer together.

- TRAINS: steam trains made America accessible and were responsible for the country's growth, improved communication, and improved trade.

- BICYCLES: mostly in large eastern cities.

- CARS: there were a few earlier, but were more common in the 1920s and after.

- ELECTRIC POWER: in homes, not common until late 1890s and early 1900s and then mostly in homes in large cities.

- PLUMBING ADVANCES: indoor plumbing and toilets for the wealthy in 1880s, but not everyone had them until the 1960s.

- MASS TRANSIT: stagecoach, train, horse-drawn omnibus off rail, on rail, and in the late 1800s, the electric trolley.

- TOILET PAPER: almost anything, pages from the Sears catalog or Farmer's Almanac. In early 1900s toilets were more common and toilet paper on a roll became more prevalent.

- COMMUNICATION: newspaper, letters, postcards, telegraph, phones were invented in 1876, but not common in homes until the 1950s, radios not common in homes until the 1920s and '30s, television didn't take off until the 1920s and '30s.

- SCHOOLS: children usually were schooled until age 14, but sometimes stopped as early as 12 or 13 if they were needed in the labor force or at home. School was held from May–August and from November–April to accommodate planting and harvesting.

- The average lifespan in 1890 was only about 45 years!

- In 1890, there were no telephones of any kind, no television, no radio, no movies, no computers, no electric lights, no electric appliances (like toasters), no microwaves, no fax machines, no scanning, no email, no cars, no planes, no speedboats. Can you imagine? That was just over 100 years ago; not that long ago, really.

Claudia Gadotti

Illustrator

I was born and raised with one brother and two sisters in Trento, Italy. I always loved books, excelled in art, and wanted to be an illustrator someday. My parents did not want me to become an artist, but a nurse, so that's what I did for a while.

Eventually, I moved to London for a year to learn English, and then went to California. There I worked as an au pair before becoming a student at the Academy of Art University in San Francisco where I graduated with a BFA in art. My professional art career started from there.

I have enjoyed illustrating children's books for sixteen years now and I also teach art part-time in a primary school. I currently make my home with my husband and two dogs in New Zealand. We have lived here for fifteen years and love it.

Kathy J Perry

Author

As a young girl, I loved reading and writing. My favorite book when I was a middle-schooler was *The Adventures of Perrine*. The historical, foreign setting attracted me. Most of all, I identified with Perrine and wanted to be like her: courageous, discerning, resourceful, and self-reliant. Written in the 1800s, it is no longer in print, but it inspired the writing of the Emeline series: *A Journey* and *Heartstrings*.

A former teacher, my reason for writing is to provide today's youth with quality stories that are relatable. I believe all stories, for good or bad, impact readers. We'll always value stories that illustrate moral character backed by biblical principles.

I'm currently "retired," but I work part-time as an administrative assistant, write, enjoy painting with watercolors, and love to bake. My husband of 42 years and I live north of the Missouri River in Kansas City, Missouri with our dog, Taz.

Read the Emeline Series

A Journey

Heartstrings

Visit KathyJPerry.com

(Find direct review links and more.)